Edie Richter is Not Alone

a novel

Rebecca Handler

The Unnamed Press
Los Angeles, CA

AN UNNAMED PRESS BOOK

www.unnamedpress.com

Unnamed Press, and the colophon, are registered trademarks of Unnamed Media LLC.

ISBN: 978-1-951213-17-6
eISBN: 978-1-951213-19-0

Line from "Dirge Without Music" by Edna St. Vincent Millay courtesy of Holly Peppe, Literary Executor, Millay Society (millay.org).

Library of Congress Cataloging-in-Publication Data

Names: Handler, Rebecca, 1973- author.
Title: Edie Richter is not alone : a novel / Rebecca Handler.
Description: First edition. | Los Angeles, CA : The Unnamed Press, [2021] | Identifiers: LCCN 2020051730 (print) | LCCN 2020051731 (ebook) | ISBN 9781951213176 (hardcover) | ISBN 9781951213190 (ebook)
Classification: LCC PS3608.A7126 E35 2021 (print) | LCC PS3608.A7126 (ebook) | DDC 813/.6--dc23
LC record available at https://lccn.loc.gov/2020051730
LC ebook record available at https://lccn.loc.gov/2020051731

Designed and Typeset by Jaya Nicely
Manufactured in the United States of America by Versa Press, Inc.

Distributed by Publishers Group West

First Edition

For Dave

Edie Richter is Not Alone

Prologue

The possum is dead. It may have been the one running back and forth across the roof at night, making a guttural purring sound, but there is no way to know for sure. It is lying in the dirt, at the foot of a thorny bush. The body strikes an unnatural pose, twisted so the head and upper limbs face the night sky. The paws look alert, mid-scratch, the fingers outstretched and the black claws like arrowheads. The dead open mouth contains sharp tawny teeth and the ears are small, round, and pink. The nose is shriveled. Its fur looks like the second-hand rabbit coat your mother kept in her closet but never wore. But this fur of this possum is not soft like a rabbit's. It is coarser, and still warm, and you discover this when you approach the lifeless animal and rest your hand on it.

You may have expected a heartbeat or a hiss, but of course you get neither. The body is quiet. You inhale.

Grab it by the tail.

You grab it by the tail and lift it from the dirt. Shaking it slightly, you see the dry soil fall off its back like brown snow. Before you can change your mind and toss it back on the ground, before you become disgusted and run inside to scrub your hands, before all of this, before all the small moments of regret become a colossal darkness, you clutch that dead possum's tail, its tendons and bone, like it is a matter of life and death and begin to run.

You are wearing the black linen sundress with the note in the pocket and you are barefoot. Strands of your limp brown hair stick to your sweaty cheeks. You position yourself behind a row of bushes and pull back your arm like a slingshot. Before you know what you are doing—

No.

It is not before you know what you are doing. It is after you know what you are doing, but before you stop it.

Now you are on the ground. Your hands are filthy. Your arm aches and your right hand, now empty, closes into a fist. You begin to shiver. You can feel your bare knees settling into the dirt and wish your whole body could get sucked into the dense darkness. An airplane roars overhead. You clench your eyes shut and force yourself to see the people inside the plane, staring at screens and drinking out of plastic cups. A man with reading glasses hanging on a string around his neck. A teenage girl traveling alone. A tired mother with a cranky toddler. A flight attendant trying to squeeze past. All of them floating in the sky.

Think about what's beyond the sky. About things that go on forever.

One October, close to Halloween, when you were young, your skin became unbearably itchy and you scratched your thighs until your sheets were streaked with blood. Your parents searched the room for bedbugs and mosquitos but came up with nothing. Your mother decided it was anxiety and your father didn't agree but said, like everything, it would pass. You took cold showers and ice baths. Your father taped your fingers with cotton balls, which only resulted in you rubbing your bare skin on the synthetic rug. Finally, they delivered you to the doctor with the hairy ears who took one look at your scarred body and announced it was scabies. The reason you can't see the bugs, he said dramatically, peering over his reading glasses, is because they are eating you from the inside. Your mother thought scabies only existed in orphanages and army barracks, so she hired professional cleaners, bought you new sheets, and swore the family to secrecy. A prescription lotion was applied, and you quickly healed.

Curled up in the dirt now, moaning, feeling your heart pounding against your rib cage, realization dawns. The secret you stuffed down is seeping out of your pores. You think this secret will kill you, that it will burst out of you and shatter your body into a million pieces. But of course you won't die, not now anyway. You will do something braver.

You will surrender.

1

My dad was acting strange long before he was diagnosed. He would leave me phone messages. Edie, it's your father, he'd say. I can't find the top to the plastic thing. I need it for the batteries. I opened all the little walls and it's nowhere. You know, Edie, it's the top to the plastic thing. It's for the batteries.

I was living in Boston, newly married, and working in marketing for an antihunger nonprofit. My parents and younger sister, Abby, were back home in San Francisco. Abby discovered thousands of black plastic coffee stirrers in Dad's bedside drawer. He bought five pairs of the same brown loafers and lined them up next to the fireplace. He was sixty-three.

Mom took Dad to a neurologist and called me. They never know for sure, she said, but it looks like Alzheimer's. I was at work, writing about a fourth grader in Detroit whose only reliable meal was a subsidized school lunch. I snuck into an empty conference room and closed the door, as Abby continued wailing in the background like she had just run over a baby. Mom went in the other room to get away from the noise. Apparently, the doctor gave him all sorts of tests like pattern recognition and basic math. He failed every one of them. He couldn't even draw a Christmas tree, Mom said.

He's Jewish, I replied, rubbing a pencil mark off the table. I worked with slobs.

I didn't think I was old enough to have a parent with Alzheimer's. Had never even considered it. The only person I knew with Alzheimer's was a former sociology professor at college. Years after he retired, he still called the department office to reserve meeting rooms. According to his former assistant, he was living in a nursing home and had bitten off most of his fingernails.

Dad got on the phone and tried to be funny. Guess what, Edie? I am crazy after all.

It's official, I told him, trying to match his tone. You're nuts.

That I am, he said.

We had nothing else to say, so I told him I loved him.

After we hung up, I returned to my desk and changed the gender of the fourth grader from a girl to a boy. Later, I went swimming at the community center near my office. Underwater, I repeated the word *Alzheimer's* over and over. I tried it in a German accent. I tried it with a lisp. I swallowed a bunch of water.

My husband, Oren, and I had plans later that night, a farewell thing for one of his colleagues, a woman with a mom name who wore cashmere cardigans and covered her mouth when she laughed. After my swim, I headed to the bar near Downtown Crossing. The room was loud, and a baseball game was on. Oren was already tipsy. I tapped him on the shoulder as he was signaling for another drink and said, My dad has Alzheimer's.

What? he said, shrugging his shoulders apologetically and pointing to the speakers in the ceiling.

Mom called, I said loudly. My dad has Alzheimer's.

She got a Weimaraner?

I leaned closer to him and spoke slowly into his ear: Alzheimer's.

Eyes bulging, he stared at me. I nodded. Oh god, Edie. Let's get out of here.

He grabbed our coats from the barstool and a moment later we were outside on Tremont Street, in the cold.

Why are we here? Oren shouted, shoving a black beanie over his head. What is wrong with you? He was drunk and suddenly very sad.

I just told you my dad has Alzheimer's.

Oren looked up at the dark sky, down at the sidewalk, and then said quietly, I know what you just told me, Edie. I just can't believe you told me here, at a bar. He shook his head and pulled me close.

We got a taxi and went home.

I wonder who drank our beer, I said, pulling my nightgown over my head.

What? said Oren, in bed, already half asleep.

Never mind, I said, flipping over my pillow to the cold side and lying down.

Oren moved closer to me and draped his arm across my chest. I love your dad, he said, and kissed my shoulder. I'm so sorry.

I wished his body could swallow mine.

*

Oren once used the phrase *meant to be* to describe the two of us. We had just had sex and I was wiping my inner thighs with his under-shirt.

Meant to be what? I asked him, as I handed him the soiled top.

Together, Edie, meant to be together. That is the only time any-one ever uses that phrase. Shaking his head in mock disbelief, he scrubbed at his lower belly.

Oren was always sure of everything and I was comfortable with him, which is not the most romantic description of our relationship but is the most accurate. We met in French class, my freshman year of college. He's two years older than I am but we're the same height. With our freckles and mouse-brown hair, people sometimes tell us we look alike, to which I respond, Yes, I suppose we do. What are my options, exactly, when someone hands me a pointless comment as if it were a gum wrapper?

The class met twice a week in the early morning. I've never minded getting up when the rest of the world is stretching its legs. My mother says it's because I was born at 4:40 A.M. The first of many inconvenient decisions you've handed to your father and me, she said.

Oren's French accent was awful. After our third or fourth class, he approached me as I was zipping up my bag and asked, in French, if I would like to go to a café with him. He had to repeat himself because I thought he was speaking Hebrew, which would not have been too much of a stretch.

Those were the days when Oren wore a yarmulke. He had eight altogether, three of which were branded—*Star Wars*, Boston Red Sox, Star of David—and five plain, in various shades of blue. He kept them on top of his dresser in two rows of four, and every morning he pinned one to his hair with a bobby pin, the kind a ballerina would wear to keep her bun in place. Once he needed new pins and asked me to pick him up a pack from the drugstore. Out of curiosity, I asked if he'd ever once bought his own pins and he admitted no, he'd take them from his mother's bedside table. Years later, when his mother died, my job was to clear out that table. There must have been two hundred bobby pins in the top drawer, along with three small jars of half-used lip balm, a handful of highlighters, a photo of Oren with his brothers, a book of matches from a restaurant called Gregg's, and a food diary. (The day before Oren's mother died she had a bowl of oatmeal, a medium glass of orange juice, two cups of black coffee, a tuna fish sandwich with one tablespoon of mayonnaise on wheat bread, a handful of stick pretzels, one apple, a small candy bar, beef stew, steamed green beans, and two glasses of red wine.) She died swerving her car to avoid a cyclist, instead hitting a traffic light head-on.

Soon after his mother's death, Oren quit wearing yarmulkes. His mother wouldn't have cared. He might have been trying to apply meaning where there was none. Anyway, he had been considering stopping for a while, as they attracted too much attention at work.

When he asked me to coffee, I said yes, mostly because I couldn't think of a good reason to say no. I was dating a fullback on the soccer team who was allergic to garlic. Oren was on again, off again with his high school girlfriend, Shiva. I used to sing, *Shiva stay or Shiva go*, on his voice mail when I couldn't reach him. It was nice—still is nice—to imagine him laughing.

I had never been to Rhode Island, where Oren grew up. He had been to San Francisco once, as part of a summer scholar program. He had eaten at the International House of Pancakes on Lombard, the one I went to after the prom. I asked him about his faith, because although I was raised Jewish, I was far from the world of yarmulkes and Israelis. He told me he believed in God but that was the extent of it. Apparently, his interest in yarmulkes was Shiva's doing, because his family, the secular Isaacson clan, treated it as you might a child's newfound vegetarianism, skeptically but without comment.

A few weeks later, after six more coffee dates and one dorm room make-out session, I broke up with Garlic and he told Shiva he had met someone else. He kept wearing the yarmulkes—they were just part of him at that point. It made no difference to me. At his graduation, I sat with his parents and his three older brothers. His mom held my hand during the ceremony. Shimon Peres was given an honorary degree. A perfect day as far as the Isaacson family was concerned.

Oren moved into an apartment in Cambridge and was promoted to senior analyst at his consulting firm. I finished up my two remaining years at college, majoring in sociology and working at the campus dry cleaners. So many disgusting comforters I had to stuff into plastic bags.

Those last two years, I lived on campus in a suite with two roommates—a math major with orange hair and his girlfriend, who smelled like calendula and was always sick. During the week, the three of us would get high and play board games. Sometimes Oren joined us but he rarely spent the night. He was an adult now with a real job. After I graduated, I did not return to California. Instead, I moved into Oren's place. My parents and sister had flown out for my graduation and stayed to help me move in. In the middle of breaking down boxes in the living room, my father pulled me aside and handed me a check for two hundred dollars. I love you, Edie, he said. Be smart.

I got a job waitressing at a fish restaurant. The manager, a South African named Raife, expected the staff to know everything about seafood, not just how it may vary in taste, but also migration patterns and catch dates. He used to manage a vitamins store and would quiz his staff on the ingredients listed on the back of protein shakes. Raife held contests each shift inspired by whatever was currently overstocked. Ok, kids, he'd say, whoever sells the most chowder gets Section A next Saturday night. Once I won for selling the most bluefish and got free movie tickets that Oren and I used two nights later. Thank you, Raife, Oren whispered as the theater lights dimmed for a war romance.

After that movie, Oren broke up with me. Walking home, he said he wasn't convinced I loved him. I called my friend Wendy, another waitress, and asked if I could stay with her for a while. Wendy was living in her parents' house in Brookline while they were in Bali for six months volunteering at an orphanage. I knew she had plenty of space. She said that was fine as long as I didn't mind her having someone over. Turns out it was Raife, and he kept me up most of the night rambling on about the restaurant owner, who was dissatisfied with the recent decline in bookings. Kid, you wouldn't believe the kind of shit I have to deal with, he said to me. I glanced behind him and gave Wendy a look. She shrugged, like no big deal. I didn't want to get into it with Wendy. It was none of my business and I was grateful she let me stay there.

The next morning, a Monday, I went back to the apartment when I knew Oren would be at work. He had left me a note:

> *Edie, thank you for understanding that I need this separation. Please don't take all of your things because I'm hopeful we'll be together again soon. Let me know if you're staying at Wendy's. Love, Oren.*

I made myself a grilled cheese sandwich and ate it standing up next to the bookshelf. I put the pan and my plate in the sink and turned on the faucet to wash them. Then I changed my mind, turned off the water, and went into the bedroom to pack. Before leaving, I circled *staying at Wendy's* on Oren's note.

Three weeks later, Oren called. Wendy and I had just gotten home from a folk music festival. I can't live without you, he said. I just need to know you love me. It's not a lot, Edie. That's all I need.

Wendy teared up and said I was lucky to have such a romantic boyfriend. I told him I'd come back in the morning. As I unpacked, hanging up my shirts in our closet, I discovered a kitten curled up on Oren's slippers. Its name was Frisbee—something dogs catch in their mouths. In the brief time we were apart, Oren had acquired a pet. Also, Oren had decided he didn't want to have children. We were making a beef stir-fry that same evening, when he said, Edie, I think kids would make our lives more complicated. What do you think?

I was dicing a red bell pepper and I agreed immediately I wanted our lives to be easy. I hadn't spent much time thinking about children. Instead I looked at him and said, I guess it could just be the two of us. Oren wiped his hands on a towel, kissed me on the neck, and asked if that would be enough for me. I said most things were more than enough for me and then he laughed in a way that sounded like he was relieved.

This decision was difficult for our families to accept. Your mother would be devastated, Oren's dad told him. I told Oren his mother was probably too busy being sad about being dead, so he shouldn't worry. Oren pointed out to his father that he's one of four sons, so the family name would live on and there would be plenty of grandchildren (in fact, at that point all of his brothers had already had at least one child). Two of his brothers were unhelpful, saying fatherhood was transformative and the best decision they ever made. His oldest brother, divorced with two children, said we were doing the right thing, that babies made everything worse. Abby, eleven at the time, said she had really wanted to be an aunt and now we had better get a dog at least. My mother told me I'd change my mind. My father said I'd always been into women's rights, whatever that meant.

Ten years passed. Our lives remained uncomplicated, easy even. I learned I had a knack for storytelling, so I stayed in marketing. I wrote the materials for a Massachusetts campaign to combat the stigma against mental illness and then an entire booklet on voting rights.

We married at Walden Pond. Thoreau didn't have children either, Oren pointed out.

Thoreau was forty-four when he died. His last two words were *moose* and *Indian*.

2

I couldn't figure out whether Dad was technically dying, but we moved from Boston to San Francisco to be closer to him. Oren had wanted to get out of the snow anyway, and he got a job at Coral, an oil company based just outside of San Francisco. I quit my marketing job and picked up some freelance work writing fund-raising letters. We got a small apartment in the inner Richmond district, three blocks from Golden Gate Park.

After Dad's diagnosis, Mom started labeling things and let Dad grow a beard. She went to a baby store and bought plastic child-protection locks for the kitchen. Just so he won't stab me, she said, as I wrestled with one of them, trying to get a corkscrew out from a drawer. You remember Tanya from my walking group? Her mother attacked the cleaning lady and they had to move her into a home.

Dad's illness was hard on Abby. She was twenty-two and living at home, trying to be a blogger. She became vegan and woke up early every morning to run five miles. She started doing most of the cooking for Mom and Dad. Mostly curry, Mom told me on the phone. I think your sister is trying to give us a permanent case of diarrhea. Not that I'm not grateful.

My sister came along when I was fourteen. Mom didn't think she could have any more children, but her body proved otherwise. One rainy night, Dad woke me up and said, We're going to the hospital to have the baby. Mrs. Whitaker's downstairs on the couch. He was home the next morning to see me off to school and said they named her Abigail and what did I think?

I told him, It matters more what she thinks. After all, it's her name.

Always the practical one, he said, pinching my arm and pulling me close. I can't wait for you to meet her.

Mom and the baby came home three days later. Abby had jaundice and needed to be kept under ultraviolet light. Jaundice is no reason to keep a baby in the hospital, Mom grumbled as she sat down carefully on the couch. As if we don't have lights in this house. Edie, be a dear and get your mother a glass of water.

Dad handed me the baby, swaddled in a blanket with blue and pink footprints, and said, Abby, meet Edie. She's your big sister.

I looked down at her red cheeks and her tiny nose. Her eyes were closed and she was wearing a lavender cap. She weighed practically nothing, a strange little animal. I felt her sigh.

How do you know she's yours and not some other baby? I asked Mom.

Dad untucked the blanket and pulled out a skinny arm to show me her wristband. See, Edie? Mom's name is on there.

My thumb and index finger fit easily around Abby's wrist. Her fingers seemed extra long. I held her hand up to my nose and inhaled. She smelled like macaroons. Then I smelled her head and kissed her on the cheek. What's for dinner, Abby? I teased. What are you going to make for us? My parents laughed in apparent relief.

My sister turned into a very talkative person. She was scatterbrained and always looked like she fell out of a ceiling fan. Mom saved a copy of a form she filled out for Abby's kindergarten teachers. Responding to the section *Tell us anything about your child that could be helpful to the teacher*, she wrote, *Chatty Patty*, and *Abby has a propensity to express her strong emotions and needs to be reminded to have more self-control.*

Abby expressed her emotions in the form of shouting and new hobbies. Now, with Dad's illness, it was cooking, mostly stews.

At first Dad wrote Post-it notes and stuck them everywhere, to the bathroom mirror, his bedside table. Two kinds of notes: explanatory— *You have problems with your memory*—and directional—*Use the blue toothbrush.* Later, the notes became *This is your house* and *Your Wife Is Louise* and *Your Children Are Edith and Abigail.*

Mom decided to sell Dad's auto-parts shop and, through a series of compelling lies, convinced Dad to sign some papers and that was that. It was purchased by a national chain of mechanics that did mostly oil changes and smog checks.

When I was growing up, Dad's longtime employee Igor used to spend a lot of time at our house. He was a gay Croatian who loved Neil Diamond and wore head-to-toe denim. He'd bring over saltwater taffy and say, All right, ladies, what's happening? He and tiny Abby would dance in the living room or we would all watch reruns. Sometimes in the middle of a show, he'd sigh wistfully and tell me what a great man my dad was. He'd say, He takes care of people, Edie.

When Mom sold the business, she asked Igor if he'd be interested in living with them and helping care for Dad. He said he'd be honored. He moved into my old room and became Dad's babysitter, always next to him, discreetly fixing things Dad would break like coffee mugs or conversations. He'd quietly apologize when Dad yelled at the pharmacist.

Mom started working part-time at a children's clothing store, thanks to a referral from Tanya from Walking Group. Mom hadn't worked in thirty years. She'd sigh with thinly veiled pride and fake grumble, They need me to come in this weekend. They're swimming in ponchos. Your dad would understand.

Whether he would or wouldn't understand wasn't important anymore. Mom liked to feel needed, and they were swimming in ponchos.

3

Most days, I drove to their house after work to spend time with Dad. Mom worked late at the store and Igor took a CPR class and went swing dancing. Abby floated in and out, and sometimes Oren brought over takeout, but mostly it was just Dad and me. When he recognized me, he'd ask questions about my health or waitressing, which of course I hadn't done for years. When he didn't know who I was, he was flirtatious. He'd say, Pretty lady, show me your smile. At first I'd remind him, Dad, it's Edie, your daughter, but that only confused him. Later I'd smile and say thank you.

He started using the word *shithead*.

Television made him anxious. He couldn't follow the story lines, and game shows made him pace. Mostly he sat in his room near the window, stroking a book or picking at his pants. Sometimes he stared at me with a fixed, infant-like stare. Other times, he stared out the window and watched the fog roll in. I stared at him and watched the fog roll in.

He was still so young.

I played his favorites: Cat Stevens, Fleetwood Mac. Sometimes he'd sing along, but mostly he just stared silently at the floor. I walked him up and down the block. He picked small purple flowers and threw them in the street. He yelled at cracks in the sidewalk.

He fell down the stairs, which were carpeted but still left bruising on his thigh. He told Mom his birthmark was sore and she told him it wasn't a birthmark, that it was a bruise, due to a fall. He said he loved her, but she was mistaken. He knew his body, he said. They had this conversation several times a day, before the bruise healed.

Mom kept his hair and nails short and donated most of his clothing to a homeless shelter. He stood in front of his now sparse closet and slid the empty hangers from one side to the other.

Abby watched videos on what to say to someone with no short-term memory and explained them to me. It's basically apologizing a lot, she said. Like, I'm sorry I made you angry. I'm sorry I embarrassed you. I'm sorry I made you feel stupid. I'm sorry this is hard. That kind of thing.

I tried it out one night. I'm sorry, Dad.

What for? He frowned and picked at the hem of his shirt.

That you're sick.

He looked at me and smiled. I'll be better soon, Edie.

I didn't know what to say. I had nothing to say.

Sometimes he went out back to play with the trash bins. Once he got stung by a bee, which left him confused for hours.

One day he looked at me and said very clearly, I feel like I am two different people.

I asked him what he meant by that but his eyes had already wandered off.

He liked going to bed. You could tell him it was getting late and he'd walk straight to the bathroom. You'd have to run after him to make sure he didn't pee in the bathtub. I brushed his teeth as he sat on the toilet, and he usually kept still if I told him a story about work. Something about a capital campaign letter I had to write or a summer camp for kids with cancer. I tried to stay away from his penis and ass, but sometimes it was unavoidable. It was important he stay clean so he could look better than he was.

Abby liked to quiz Dad. An end-of-life review. She asked him his favorite memory from his childhood, the names of the last three presidents, how he felt the day she was born.

He could not name any presidents, but he could recall, with startling precision, the time he was asked to recite one of Shakespeare's sonnets in school and remembered only the first line. It was a memory about forgetting. He repeated this often for a while.

We learned from the neurologist that when Dad repeated a story, we should respond as if it were the first time we were hearing it. This neurologist never remembered our names, wore her long brown hair in a French braid, and always had a woven purple purse strapped across her white coat. I once asked her what she kept in her purse, and she looked at me strangely and said, My wallet, my phone, nothing special. I asked her why she carried a purse—didn't they have lockers in this hospital? I told her I'd never seen a doctor with a purse before and she said maybe I hadn't met enough female doctors and I said, No, that's not it. Abby elbowed me and Mom said, Never mind. Dad laughed. He didn't know where he was.

After several falls, he gave up walking and allowed Igor to lift him in and out of a wheelchair. He started to lose weight. He stopped speaking, except for the occasional stutter that was usually accompanied by pointing at something. Ma, ma, ta, ta.

With the disappearance of speech came the arrival of pain. He would howl suddenly, as if he were a dog and someone was at the door. This would frighten everyone. Abby would cry. Igor would panic. He wasn't trained for this. Finally, Mom called hospice. This doesn't mean he's dying, she said. We just need more help. And he gets six months paid for.

A heavyset woman who smelled like pine and jasmine started coming over every day, except occasionally when another woman came. The other woman didn't look much older than Abby and she had an eyebrow piercing. No one liked her. The heavyset woman told me that caring for a sick family member causes a sharp increase in blood pressure, blood sugar, and cortisol, which can affect decision-making.

One day when she was cleaning him, I asked her if he was dying. She motioned for me to join her in the hallway.

It's best to not talk about that in front of him, she said, rubbing my arm.

She smelled like a sachet you'd toss in your underwear drawer. I took a step back.

At this point, we're not sure what he understands, she said.

Oren sometimes cried after seeing Dad. He said watching someone deteriorate like this wasn't fair to anyone. It's like a bridge coming down, he whispered one night in the dark.

Everyone wanted to know if Dad still recognized me. The postman, the lady in the locker room, Mrs. Whitaker.

Wendy called one night as I was driving home from Dad's. She was eating an apple. Does he know who you are? she asked, her mouth full.

I think so, I told her. He asks me how work is going.

But he'd ask anyone that, right? she said, munching.

It's hard to tell, I said. I didn't feel like talking about it. I pulled into a gas station.

When Dad was healthy, he began each day with a glass of orange juice. Sunshine in a glass, he called it. Mom disagreed. More like diabetes in a glass. She was anti-juice, but he didn't care. When oranges were cheap, he would squeeze them himself, using this simple plastic juicer he picked up at a garage sale. He would rotate each half exactly four times before tossing it in the sink. When oranges were more expensive, he would buy a jug of the generic kind. This of course was not nearly as delicious, but he would say it got the job done.

When he was sick, I brought him juice, sometimes sneaking it in if Mom was in a mood. Orange juice wouldn't kill him of course. Swallowing liquids became more difficult, so Oren had the idea to add cornstarch to his glass and spoon-feed him. We tasted it first and decided it wasn't bad. Oren said it tasted like a lukewarm snow cone.

One day Dad couldn't figure out the spoon. He would pucker his lips but wouldn't take it in his mouth. Come on, Dad, I said, and took a spoonful myself. But still, all he could manage was a tentative imitation of a fish. I deposited a small morsel of the wet sand on his bottom lip and told him to lick it off, but it wobbled around and eventually dropped on his shirt.

Finally, I put the spoon down on his bedside table and dunked my index finger in the glass. I tapped my finger on his lips and felt the flicker of his tongue. With my finger in his mouth, he gave me a goofy look, like a baby tasting ice cream. I shook my head and said, Well, that's one way to do it. That day, Dad sucked his glass of orange juice off my finger.

I knew Dad would stop recognizing me. I didn't know I would stop recognizing him.

I'm always looking for clues and memorizing faces, storing them for another time. I'm not crazy. I know no one's going to stop me on the street and ask me whether I've seen anyone with chipped nails. People and their habits feel useful to me in a way I can't explain. Oren once said I search through people the way you'd search through a cereal box for the prize. I told him I don't think they put prizes in cereal anymore and he told me it was just an example.

Telling someone else's story is easy. You focus on one detail and it sticks with people, makes the subject more memorable, more appealing. It is different when it comes to your own story. You can't see the thing that stands out, the quality that makes you different from every other person. You certainly feel different, but your perception of yourself is too skewed to count for anything. You can never know what it's like to talk to you, what it's like to walk next to you, or what it feels like to touch you. You never really see yourself. You project your bits out into the world for everyone to collect like shells. You belong to everyone.

*

Sometimes when we were alone, I'd peer into Dad's eyes and search for what was left. He might like to hear you're ok, the heavyset woman had told me once.

Dad? I said, searching his face. Just so you know, I'm ok. Igor's ok. Mom's ok. Abby is pretty upset but she'll be ok.

His eyes looked cloudy and he smelled vaguely of pee.

You're doing a good job, I said. I wondered why I added that and patted him on his shoulder bone.

Some days I didn't know what to do with Dad, so I sat on the floor and watched the heavyset woman embroider. She made mostly bookmarks and wallets, with flowers or geometric patterns. She offered to teach me but I said I preferred to watch. She began each new color by making a big knot that she would snip off after completing several stitches. It's called a waste knot, she explained. Sometimes you have to make a mess before you straighten everything out.

Abby emailed me an article about turmeric and how it's meant to prevent dementia. Too late, I wanted to say at first. But then I realized she meant us.

Oren helped the heavyset woman attach a railing to the bed, and we bought foam pillows in a variety of shapes and sizes. Mrs. Whitaker gave us a pillow with a Jane Austen quote. *There is nothing like staying at home for real comfort.* This one we kept between his thighs to help with chafing.

Igor learned how to administer morphine. This involved droplets under the tongue. It reminded me of when I once used a syringe to feed a newborn flying squirrel at a zoo summer camp. The squirrel was swaddled in a navy-blue washcloth and I told the camp counselor it looked like a baby space alien. She scratched its tiny head and said, Can you believe what Mother Nature creates? The counselor had one green eye and one brown eye.

Often, Dad was constipated and his stomach became rock hard and bloated. I watched a video on abdominal massage and tried it out on Oren. He told me it tickled and I had better leave abdominal massage to the experts. The heavyset woman sometimes had to extract Dad's poo with a catheter. She said it didn't bother her at all; on the contrary, she liked the idea of relieving some of his pain. Plus, she added, the poo smell is better than open sores. We call those dank and stank, she said, laughing.

Dad's skin became paper-thin, like stretched cotton, and looked like it was floating above his body. He looked like he could shed. Like one day I'd come in and there would just be a big pile of skin on the bed. The heavyset woman massaged his hands and feet with pink lotion that came in a gallon-sized bottle that said NEW! FRESH SCENT! There were rashes and raised sores and red dry spots, each requiring its own ointment. She counted his sores daily and logged them in a red notebook.

Mom's side of the bed was now covered with baby wipes, changing pads, and creams. At a glance it looked like the beginning of life, something to celebrate. She said she felt like someone stole him from us. Soon after, she began sleeping in the den.

In second grade, the teacher instructed us to draw a rainbow and then cover it with black crayon. We unfolded paper clips and scraped over the black, revealing slivers of color. I took my drawing home and stuffed it behind the bookshelf. It wasn't a rainbow at all anymore.

One day after visiting Dad, I went to the mall to buy shoes. As I waited for the salesman to bring out my size, one thought came rushing into my head like a terrorist. *Everyone at this shoe store is going to die.* I ran back to my car and drove west, to the ocean. It was unusually still. The waves were small and the fog lingered above the water. Everything was waiting for something.

Eventually Dad stopped eating. Not long after, I killed him.

4

Oren had asked me recently how I was holding up. I had just come back from seeing Dad and had collapsed on the couch. He brought me a glass of wine and rubbed my back. I couldn't answer him. It could have been the phrase *holding up* that I was stuck on. Later I heard him whispering on the phone with his father. She won't talk about any of it, Dad. I don't know what to do.

One night after helping the heavyset woman give Dad a bath, I left to meet Oren at a Mexican place where piñatas hung from the ceiling and the walls were plastered with framed photos of famous athletes. While we waited for a table, Oren struck up a conversation with a couple, also waiting to eat. The man was wearing a black fleece jacket with a bird logo. Oren asked him if he worked at a tech company, the one with the bird. The man's girlfriend interjected. We both work there, she said. It's how we met. They were put on a project together, making it easier for people to use their phones to check news updates. Oren knew more about this phone feature than I did. He always seemed to know enough to help a conversation move forward. My eyes traveled to the ceiling, where in the corner near the window was a stuffed toy parrot hanging by its neck on a cord of half-broken Christmas lights.

The man asked Oren what he did for a living and Oren said he worked in oil. Sorry? The man didn't understand. Oren said he worked for Coral. The man and the woman nodded silently until the woman asked Oren how he could work for an oil company when they, the oil companies, were killing the earth. I mean, what do you tell your children? Do you have children?

Did you drive here?

Oren looked at me. I hadn't spoken in a while. The couple looked at me. I stared at the woman and repeated myself. Did you drive here?

Yes, she said, crossing her arms over her chest. Is that an oil reference?

Yes, it is, I responded. Everyone loves to hate oil companies, but then they get in their cars or turn on the heat. It's ridiculous.

She glared at me and said, That's not fair.

My voice rising, I said, You're right. It's not fair.

It's ok, Edie, Oren said, resting his palm on my back. He told the woman that many people in San Francisco seemed to feel that way about Coral. We're not very popular, he joked. He was trying to make her feel better about saying something rude.

On the way to our table, I glanced over at the stuffed parrot hanging from the ceiling and thought about hypocrites. Then I thought about how the past two years had been a staggeringly slow sequence of staring, washing, holding, pacing, and wiping. Oren and I spent most weekends with Dad, cleaning the skin between his fingers and toes and watching him drift in and out of consciousness.

Our food arrived and Oren reached for my hand across the table. Don't let it bother you so much, he said. Oil is problematic.

Unlike tech companies, I said, rolling my eyes.

He smirked and said, I love it when you defend me. He looked down at his plate, overflowing with black beans and diced tomatoes, and said, This city is nuts.

There was a bird hanging by its neck in this restaurant. No one was doing anything. Nothing was getting done.

The first bite burned my mouth, but after that, it was delicious.

5

If you were to ask me all about it, I guess I'd say it ended up as something really big but started out as something really small, if I were to say anything at all about it. I didn't plan on killing my father. In fact, I don't even like to put it that way. I didn't plan on ending my father's life, if you can call it a life when a person has essentially become a thing. But an idea can appear like a new freckle and become a cancer.

The sun had already set by the time I arrived. Walking up the stairs to the house, I stopped to pick up the mail: a wicker furniture catalog, something from the symphony, and a couple of bills. The house smelled like garlic. Abby had a stew on and was also preparing a pasta sauce to freeze. By this point, she had become obsessed with ingredients and their purported benefits, as if antioxidants and vitamin E would save us all.

Mom was reading in Dad's bedroom, in the chair near the window. Oh good, you're here, she said as she removed her reading glasses. I was hoping to stretch my legs.

How is he? I asked as I unzipped my leather jacket and dumped my purse on the foot of his bed.

Same.

It's a little cold out, maybe wear a scarf.

Thanks, Edie. She touched my shoulder. You staying for dinner?
I shrugged my shoulders and closed the bedroom door behind her. I heard her say goodbye to Abby and leave the house.

Dad's cheeks were sunken in, and the spaces created by his collarbones were like two tiny swimming pools. His mouth was open and his lips looked gray and dry. Until a couple of months ago, Igor was still dressing Dad in polo shirts and khakis, which gave the impression he was planning on going in to work after a quick nap. The heavyset woman and the one with the eyebrow piercing spent lots of time undressing and redressing him. Now, he was in hospital gowns full time. Easier to clean him.

I walked the periphery of the room, past the stacks of adult diapers and wipes, past Dad's leather reading chair, his closet, and the window overlooking the neighbors' brick patio and rusty furniture. I stopped at his dresser and looked at all the pill bottles lined up in rows like orange soldiers: lorazepam for anxiety, haloperidol for nausea and agitation, suppositories for constipation, and something called prochlorperazine maleate. I picked up the atropine sulfate and read the instructions. Two pills every two hours for the actively dying patient. Do not drive or operate heavy machinery while taking this medication.

I looked in the mirror. My limp brown hair hung plainly on either side of my tired face. My lips were chapped and a pimple was forming smack in the center on my chin.

I ran my hand across the top of the shiny dresser. Dad had made this years ago and had filed it down perfectly. It was smooth and warm. The room was kept hot these days. He barely had any body fat left and any gust of air would run right through him.

Seven syringes of morphine, monitored by the heavyset woman, were stowed in the Simon and Garfunkel mug I gave Dad for Father's Day. According to her, morphine was to be used only if the patient was clearly in pain.

I opened his top drawer. Socks and underwear. Mom had forgotten about these drawers. The second one was t-shirts. On top of the pile was a light blue one that said JESUS IS COMING, LOOK BUSY! I remembered this shirt. He wore it on a flight to Boston one time, revealing it midflight when he took off his sweatshirt. Mom was beside herself. At dinner that night, she said in disbelief, Can you believe what your father wore? On an airplane, for goodness' sake. She took a bite of a hot dinner roll and said, People don't have normal senses of humor on airplanes, Paul. They don't want to hear jokes about Jesus.

I sat down on the bed next to him, holding the shirt. He smelled like stale orange juice and rubbing alcohol.

What if he had opened his eyes or let out a little snort? What if he had given me a sign that he had heard me? Would things have worked out differently?

All I can say is what happened next.

I wrapped part of the t-shirt around my left hand and covered the mouth on my father's body. With my right hand, I pinched the nostrils. The body constricted slightly. I closed my eyes, pretending they were sewn shut, and forced myself to think of anything else.

I thought of Mom and the book on the afterlife that she had just purchased online. I thought of Igor and how he missed his sister's wedding in Croatia last year to stay with Dad. I thought of all the pills, the appointments, and the mountain of paperwork.

I felt a tremor and pushed down harder on the mouth and nostrils. I kept my eyes closed. This should just take a minute, I said quietly, as if I were a person who walked around ending lives willy-nilly and knew exactly how long it would take. As if I were a person who had done this before.

I thought of Abby. All of her calls and her crying. The way she now used the word *heavy* to describe her feelings.

Now I could smell her stew. Maybe it was the one with carrots and what's the other thing that looks like a carrot? Turnip? No, it wasn't turnip. I squeezed the nose tighter and pushed down on the open mouth. His legs made small jerking movements, and a hand popped up against my thigh. I would not open my eyes. Do not open your eyes.

Parsnip.

When I was six, I helped Dad paint a bookshelf on a tarp in our driveway. He built it himself, the first of many bookshelves he ended up making. I watched him carefully paint it for an hour or so until he offered me a brush and said, Your little fingers can get in there and do the fine detail. I remember the smell of the paint and the way the blue darkened as it dried. Dad painted whiskers on my cheeks, and I insisted on keeping them for a couple of days. My helper, he'd say as he stroked my cheek before bed.

He and I used to go out Sunday mornings to pick up donuts. A coffee roll for Mom, a jelly donut for Abby, and four chocolate glazed for Dad and me (two to eat there, two to bring home). Donut World was open twenty-four hours and there were always a few customers who looked like they had been there all night, sitting in the corner drinking coffee out of Styrofoam cups. Dad thought it was a crime that they offered coffee flavors like hazelnut and vanilla, and he'd joke about it with the manager. Still got that garbage coffee I see, he'd say with the smile he reserved only for ladies behind counters. Your dad's a real charmer, the manager would fake groan as she handed me a powdered donut hole.

The body hadn't moved in a while now. I removed my thumb and forefinger from the nose and sat there for a while with my eyes closed, my other hand still over the mouth. The only sound was the ticking clock on his bedside table. I opened my eyes and blinked twice. The sight of my wrapped hand over his mouth startled me, like when you wake up to find your arm has fallen asleep. For a moment it appeared to belong to someone else. I pulled it away quickly, unwrapped my hand, and tossed the t-shirt on the floor.

Wendy had been at her grandmother's bedside when she died. The whole family had gathered, at the grandmother's request, and Wendy said that at the moment of death, she and her mother both felt a breeze blow through their hair. And the windows were closed, she had told me in disbelief, completely closed.

There was no breeze in Dad's bedroom at the time of his death. But I knew he was dead because he finally looked alive. His eyes were now open, bloodshot and still, and he looked calm, like someone watching pigeons. Now absent, his previous tiny movements seemed larger.

I picked the shirt off the floor and returned it to the drawer, my legs and hands shaking.

I swiped my jacket and bag from the foot of the bed and walked to the door. I turned around and looked at Dad lying there, watching the birds. I hadn't noticed his hair until now. It was shiny and damp. Mom must have styled it with a wet brush, something Dad used to do when he got home from work. He called it a French shower.

I walked into the kitchen. How is he? Abby said. She was filling water glasses.

Not staying, I mumbled, and quickly left the house. I felt like I might throw up. When I was about halfway home, my phone rang. I pulled over in front of the dry cleaners that displayed photos of its customers on the walls. Recently they had lost my gray wool coat and I asked them to take down my picture.

I took a breath and answered the call. Mom was panicked. Come back, Edie. You have to come home. I hung up without saying a word and turned the car around.

I stood in the doorway as if watching a play unfold. Abby was lying next to Dad, sobbing. Mom must have called the heavyset woman before she called me, because she was here now, pacing back and forth at the foot of Dad's bed.

The heavyset woman was dumbfounded because she didn't guess he was so close, but also somewhat pleased because, as she said, clearly he didn't want to put all of you through this any longer.

Mom made me a list and I made a bunch of calls. There would be no autopsy of course. He was very sick.

The funeral went smoothly enough, despite the fact that I woke up with a stomachache and wore the wrong shoes for walking in dirt. My old neighbor friend showed up, which was a surprise because my dad once called her mother a conniving bitch and that ended our friendship. I told a few stories about Dad, and then Igor spoke, which no one was expecting. Abby cried a lot. Oren held my hand. Everyone said Dad would have been proud.

Later that night, soon after Oren and I got home, he asked if I minded that he go to sleep but said he'd be happy to stay up if I needed him. I didn't need him. I didn't know what I needed.

My shoes were filthy from the graveyard, so I stood over the kitchen sink and scrubbed them with the dish sponge. I flipped the wet shoes over on the counter and rinsed the sink. The dirt mixed with old pieces of rice and diced tomatoes, and I stared at the drain until it all washed away.

I did it.

I flipped on the light in the bathroom and stared at myself in the mirror. *It was me.* I closed my eyes and rubbed my fingertips over my eyeballs.

After brushing my teeth, I returned to the living room and collapsed in the green chair, the crushed velvet one that Oren bought at a garage sale soon after we moved to San Francisco. He carried it up the stairs and declared proudly that it was a rescue chair, as if it were a pit bull mix. I told him it was the ugliest thing I had ever seen. He told me it was ugly because it didn't have anything to prove, and I should just stop talking and sit down. He was right. It was a very comfortable chair.

My phone buzzed. It was a text from Abby: *I miss him. Even the sick version.*

I suffocated him, I didn't say. What would Abby think? Mom? My glands hurt.

I turned off my phone and stared at the ceiling. The streetlight streaming through the window blinds cast a shadow that looked just like an enormous feather. Someone outside honked a horn, perhaps picking up that teenage boy next door. It seemed too late for honking, but I didn't have the energy to say anything to anyone. I didn't feel like much of anything.

The cat was licking its front paw at the foot of the bed and Oren was sound asleep. He was curled up in a ball, his back toward me. I slowly pulled the sheet out from under him and rested my palm on his back. The coolness of my hand made him twitch, but he quickly returned to his other world. I felt his body inhale and exhale and tried to match his breathing. It was no use. I couldn't slow my breath down. I rolled over on my back and tried to be as still as possible.

We buried Dad naked, wrapped in a shroud, a Jewish custom. I had never seen the cloth they used and wondered if it was tough like burlap or soft like cotton. Obviously it wouldn't have made a difference to anyone. I tried to name all the ingredients in Abby's stew, and somewhere after bay leaf, I fell asleep.

6

The day after the funeral, Igor moved out. *Staying with friends for a while,* he texted. *Of course,* I wrote back. *Thank you for your help.*

Two weeks later, Abby and I sat cross-legged in our parents' bedroom and separated Dad's clothes and knickknacks into three categories: keep, trash, and donate/Igor. Mom had a sale at work. It's accessories season, she said, outlining her lips with a brown pencil. For children? I asked. For everyone, she said, exasperated, and tossed her purse over her shoulder and left the house.

Abby pinched Dad's boxers, scrunched up her nose, and said, Edie, promise me when I die, you'll throw out my underwear without touching them.

Wouldn't I have to touch them in order to throw them out?

Use tongs or something.

Kitchen tongs? Then I'd have to throw those out too.

She sighed and tossed them in a black garbage bag. She stretched her legs out in front of her and bent over to touch her toes. She has always been so flexible and bendy. Even when she was tiny, she'd grab her ankles and shove them behind her head while Dad would cringe and Mom would try to imitate her. She muttered something I didn't understand.

Couldn't hear you, I said.

She lifted her head and was crying.

What's wrong?

Her eyes looked like veiny shrimp. Our dad died, Edie, that's what's wrong. She sounded frustrated and grabbed the remaining underwear pile and shoved all of it deep into the bag. She turned her head to look at the pile of socks on the rug and cried, What do we do with the socks?

What do you mean?

She reached over, grabbed one black pair in each hand, and shook her fists back and forth. I mean what do we do with the stupid socks, Edie? Some of them are basically brand new, and he wasn't wearing these anyway. He wore those nasty light blue hospital socks, the ones Regina brought over. She wiped her nose on her hoodie.

The heavyset woman's name was Regina. I remember when she gave us those socks. She said the elastic wasn't as tight and wouldn't bother him as much.

Abby took a deep breath and said slowly, We could donate them, right? Or give them to Igor?

I didn't know Dad had been bothered by his socks. I hadn't considered this.

Abby was now glaring at me. She knew I wasn't listening to her. Just tell me what to do, she said, looking at her hands one at a time. She screamed, What. Do. We. Do. With. The. Socks!

She flung them across the room, one at a time. The first one hit the closet door and ricocheted back, and the second one flew behind the bed. She stood up and over me, her hands on her hips. The zipper on her jeans was down.

And you, Abby said, her voice growing increasingly shrill. You haven't done anything all day. You've been sitting there, watching me touch Dad's disgusting boxer shorts and making weird mindless comments.

I've hauled four huge bags down to the garage already, and you haven't even offered to help. What do you even think about any of this? Do you want any of his stuff? How am I supposed to figure this out? Why isn't Mom here?

Abby inhaled and screamed, Since when do accessories have a season?

She was angry. And she was right. I wasn't doing anything, so I left.

That night Oren made a chicken dish requiring four heads of garlic. When we sat down to eat, he told me it might need salt and that Coral had offered him a one-year position in Perth, Australia, and of course he would turn it down because the timing was really bad, but he wanted to tell me anyway because it meant that he was doing well at work.

Let's do it, I said.

Go to Perth? Are you sure? He was shocked.

I took a bite of the chicken, told him it was delicious and yes, I was sure. After dinner we pulled out his mom's giant atlas that we kept under the couch because it was too big for a shelf and turned to the index. Perth, Australia, was between Pertek, Turkey, and Perth, Ontario. We turned to the Australia page. Each of the six states was a different shade of brown or green. Perth sat alone on the west coast, in a time-out from the rest of the country.

Wow, it's really nowheresville, I said to Oren.

He put his arm around me. We would leave in a month, Edie. Are you sure you want to live in Australia?

I said, Where wouldn't I live for a year besides somewhere with suicide bombers or strip malls?

He didn't think this was funny.

*

Three separate people sent me the same YouTube video of two kangaroos boxing in an Australian suburb. One of my clients at an organization for blind people sent me an article about snake attacks in Western Australia and another one about spiders. And then he said he was sorry to hear about my dad and asked if I'd write an annual appeal letter for them before I left.

I wrote a great letter to old people in wealthy zip codes, suggesting they think about visually impaired people when they write up their wills. Organizations for the blind typically receive most of their money from dead people, something I had recently learned from an article in *Philanthropy Today*. The letter was in large font with a return envelope featuring a stamp with a guide dog. It was perfection.

Of course Abby cried when I told her we were moving, but later that night, she emailed me a link to a health food store in Perth. Turmeric lattes, Edie! Jealous! She said she would take Frisbee.

Mom said in a whisper that I should go. That the change could be good for me. I had been acting differently since Dad died. We all grieve in our own ways, she said. I can't believe you killed him, she didn't say.

I received an email from someone named Brenda, the housing and lifestyle coordinator at Coral. She was there to make sure our move went smoothly and if there was anything, anything at all, feel free to reach out any time. She arranged for some of our belongings to be sent in advance, whatever we wanted to bring with us, and everything else to be put in storage. On a Wednesday morning, three men—two short, one tall—showed up with back braces and enormous rolls of bubble wrap. The tall man wrapped the ugly chair first in plastic, then in brown paper, and secured the whole thing with rope. It looked like a birthday present for a giant. By four o'clock, I was sitting on our front steps icing my ankle with a cold pack given to me by one of the short men. I had fallen down the stairs, after a last-minute errand to the pharmacy so I could give the men twelve bottles of ibuprofen, which they then jammed into the box filled with clothing, duck figurines, and a vase in the shape of an owl. Everything I owned, with the exception of one packed suitcase and a backpack, was now wrapped up like mummies.

Oren brought home a bottle of champagne. It was New Year's Eve.

The next week, we boarded a flight to the end of the world.

7

The flight attendant handed me an Australian newspaper. Our compliments, she said with her bright red lipstick.

The front-page story was about Australia's immigration policy. The government was telling desperate people on boats to turn back and entire families were drowning. They were transferring people to islands near Papua New Guinea.

I looked over at Oren. We were seated in business class, compliments of Coral. He was poking the touchscreen monitor, scrolling through movies. Last-minute passengers were boarding, and flight attendants were taking coats and offering drinks and newspapers.

I took a sip of sparkling water and thought about the words *asylum seeker*. Out the window, men in bright orange vests rushed around in the dark like fireflies. It was almost midnight and our flight to Sydney would last fifteen hours. There we would board an additional flight across the country to Perth.

A woman across the aisle was reading a book with an orange cover called *A Whole New Mind*. She had a tattoo on her ankle that looked like the word *lying* in cursive. I spotted it when we boarded. Now, with her ankle resting on her knee, I had a clearer view and realized it was a squiggly shape followed by the word *ying*.

Oren reached over and squeezed my arm. You're so far away, he said. That's the only problem with these seats. He smiled. He was wearing a dark blue fleece jacket because he was always freezing on planes.

How long is it to Perth from Sydney? I said, yawning.

Four or five hours, he said.

The flight attendant collected our glasses and tiny bowls of warm cashews.

Seems like a long time from now, I said, buckling my seat belt.

Edie?

Yup.

Thanks for this, Oren said.

Something beeped overhead.

For what? I said.

He touched my hand and said, For doing this move. I think it's gonna be great.

Me too, I said, and looked out the window. I rolled the words *furnace* and *thermos* around in my mouth.

I had no idea how anything was going to go. After everything with Dad, all the plans and logistics had been made in a fog. I was needed for some decisions, but most seemed to happen without my involvement. That was fine with me.

It was a clear night and the moon was full. I thought about something Abby had emailed me. In 1962, John Glenn was orbiting Earth in his spaceship. When people in Perth learned he would be passing over their city at night, they turned on all their lights. Families stood outside in the dark waving flashlights, and skyscrapers stayed lit up. Nestled between the Indian Ocean and desert, Perth's isolation became a gift of a sort. For a time, Perth was known as the City of Lights.

We took off.

8

Out of all the airports I had been to, Perth's certainly had the most people wearing flip-flops. There was a shirtless man waiting at baggage claim. He wore a backward baseball cap, which reminded me of Oren's college roommate who smelled like charcoal. Mom would have wondered if this was the best he could do. We waited in the airport taxi line across from a billboard with a close-up of a woman's black eye. WELL, HE SAID HE WAS SORRY. CALL THE DOMESTIC VIOLENCE HELP LINE.

It's hot, I said to Oren as he squatted and searched his bag for our house address.

We need to start speaking in Celsius, he said, laughing, popping up with a folder marked PERTH. Oren got immense pleasure from his label maker.

I had expected that the cars would look different, smaller, like in Europe. They didn't. They just looked like they were driving themselves because no one was sitting where they ought to be. Posters declaring REAL AUSTRALIANS SAY WELCOME were stuck to lampposts and deserted buildings.

Perth looked flatter than I had pictured. If it weren't for all the billboards, I could have seen for miles. We stayed on the same road for a long time, passing faded pink, blue, and brown buildings, mostly fast-food places and strip malls. Domino's, McDonald's, something called Hungry Jack's that looked like Burger King, a chain called Red Rooster. I saw at least three adult sex shops on that road, triple-X-video-looking places, and wondered if people were still renting DVDs here. I lost count of plastic surgery clinics. Before and after photos of women's bellies and thighs overlooked the main road like clouds of cellulite.

Then a forest appeared on the left. Just like that. It was as if someone had just turned the channel, just clicked over to something else entirely. Muted shades of green and gray continued all the way up the street.

Kings Park, Oren said. We must be almost home.

I stuck my head out the window, closed my eyes, and inhaled deeply. The air smelled like fire, eucalyptus, and car exhaust, a surprisingly pleasant combination. The taxi stopped and I opened my eyes. We were at a red light. On the corner, overlooking the street, was an enormous billboard with an overly tan man wearing too much hair gel. He was dressed in a tuxedo, but only had a torso and a head. The rest of him was made to look like a chess piece, and next to his picture was the phrase THE BEST INVESTMENT MOVE YOU'LL MAKE. It was very unnerving to see half a man like that, to see him smile even though he has no arms or legs. Half person, half chess piece. I locked eyes with him as we drove off.

We passed a mortuary called Chipper Funerals, took a couple of turns down tree-lined streets, and pulled into a short brick driveway. Brenda, the housing and lifestyle coordinator, had sent us photos of the house soon after Oren had accepted the position. Red brick with white trim and stained-glass windows, the house would best be described as quaint. A crafty aunt's house.

I stepped out of the car and looked around. An ibis was perched on a baby stroller in the driveway of the house next door. Its long, curved black beak looked prehistoric and daunting. I thought about showing Oren, but I was too tired to speak. Stretching my arms over my head, I spotted a single tiny cloud in an otherwise empty sky. It looked left behind.

The key was under the welcome mat, on a purple key chain with an anchor logo that said FREMANTLE DOCKERS. A dock laborers' union? I stared at the key until Oren said, Go on in, Edie. See if you can find the air-conditioning.

The house smelled faintly of cat litter and the box that was packed in San Francisco was in the entryway. This left me momentarily confused.

Three bedrooms were too many, but we could always just leave a couple of doors closed. I passed one with a chalkboard wall, where someone had written *Welcome, Oren and Edie*. I found the master bedroom near the kitchen. The heavy curtains were halfway closed. A sunbeam shone like a spotlight against the dresser, and the room was stifling. I noticed an air-conditioning unit in one of the upper corners and, after some searching, located its controller on the wall near the closet. I turned it on to full blast and stood directly under it, where the cool air could blow on the back of my neck. I lifted my shirt and turned to face it.

Brenda had arranged furniture, cheap-looking stuff. I was now facing the bed and counted the pillows. I took three steps forward and collapsed face-first on two of them. When I awoke, the sunbeam had disappeared and, in fact, the room was dark. Someone had closed the bedroom door. Disoriented, I wiped the drool off the side of my mouth, stumbled into the hallway, and called out for Oren.

Out here!

Where are you?

Past the kitchen. Out back.

The kitchen was dark except for the glow of the oven light. Something smelled good. I opened the screen door and stumbled out into the dark, into what sounded like the world's largest cricket convention. What time is it? I asked.

Almost eight. You slept all afternoon. Oren was sitting back in a wooden chair, feet propped on the chair in front of him. He was drinking a beer and on his laptop. YouTube was open, a stand-up comedian.

Why didn't you wake me up? I'm hungry, I said, rubbing my eyes.

There's lasagna warm for you in the oven. Brenda froze one for us. How nice is that?

The lights were on in the building behind our house. I could see a desk and an office chair on the second floor.

It's a nursing home, Oren said, clicking play. You gotta see this, Edes. He motioned toward his screen. It's that religious guy with all the kids.

I gotta pee.

Toilet paper's on the floor, there's no holder thingy.

Sitting on the toilet, I put my head in my hands. I felt nauseated. I couldn't remember the last time I was this tired. I rubbed my eyes.

Oren soon went to bed and I ate Brenda's lasagna outside in the dark. I took a shower, unpacked the moving box, and lined up my duck figurines on the kitchen windowsill. I took a sleeping pill and joined Oren in bed. He had shut off the air-conditioning and was naked and sticky under the covers, so I rolled out of bed and turned it back on. I lay coverless, staring at a vent near the ceiling that looked like the outline of two lion cubs touching noses. I finally fell asleep.

I woke up at two in the morning to an incessant scratching sound in the bedroom wall and occasional moaning and growling. For a few seconds I didn't know where I was and desperately scanned the dark room for hints of recognition. It was impossible not to think of Dad. Was this how it had felt for him in the beginning? Had he woken up panicked in the middle of the night, hearing things? For a moment, was the person next to him a stranger? I wondered if there was anything at all that would have helped him calm down, or if all he could have done was wait. Would he have trusted the stranger next to him, or would he have begun to recognize her after a while? Every thought was so fleeting by then, so temporary.

If I had to rely on Oren for reminders of who and where I was, it's hard to know whether I'd buy whatever truth he was selling. I don't know if I would have believed it. It's one thing to spin a story, and it's another thing entirely to fall for it.

9

The doorbell rang.

Edie, is it?

Jamie, the driving instructor. Oren had convinced me to book a lesson. He was worried about me driving on the other side of the road. Opening the door, I grimaced as I inhaled. After one week in Perth, I remained startled by the strength and frequency of the smell of smoke in the mornings. Oren said it was prescribed burning in Kings Park. Setting fires to control fires.

Jamie's voice had been chipper on the phone, but here was a weathered man on the other side of the screen door, deep wrinkles on his forehead and dark freckles on his nose. He tucked in the back of his blue polo shirt, which had a small logo on the front. SAFE DRIVING WA. Red letters inside of a yellow sun. In addition to his wrinkled skin and receding hairline, Jamie also had the potbelly of an older man.

This one's broken, he said, fiddling with the door hinge. You got a screwdriver? Happy to pop that back in for you.

I retrieved the screwdriver and rejoined him on the porch.

He pulled a pair of reading glasses out of his front pocket. He didn't seem like the type to wear delicate black plastic frames perched on the end of his nose. They made him look like a watchmaker. Let's see, he said, facing the screen door. My sister's got one just like this one and it's busted all the time. From years of kids banging it back and forth. You got kids? He examined the hinge and started picking at it with his fingers.

No.

At that moment, a baby cried somewhere nearby. Jamie laughed and said, Good on you. Blessings, of course, but they just break everything. Not sure why they still make screen doors since kids are around. No point. And they've often got a couple redbacks on 'em too. You gotta watch for those, Edie.

I was watching three magpies peck at the weeds on our front patio. Then I heard a woman's voice call out: Benny, where's the esky?

The voice came from next door, where the large stroller remained parked out front.

Jamie pointed at the magpies, And that lot? Be careful, they dive at you. They'll bite you in the face if you get too close to their little ones.

I cringed.

Well, you're gonna need a couple more a these, he said, depositing two rusty screws in the palm of my hand. There's the problem. Those need to be replaced. You got any here?

I promised we'd pick up some new ones and asked if we could get started with the lesson.

Give 'em here, he said, holding out his hand. I'll hold on to 'em and we'll make a stop at Bunnings. We gotta drive anyway, right? Might as well make the most of it. Jamie grinned, shoved the screws along with his glasses in his pocket. Just be careful here with this door. He opened and closed it gently a few times, demonstrating how to use a broken door. You ready, Edie?

Do I need anything?

Just a prayer and a sense of humor, he said. You'll be all right. Besides, car has extra brakes, so I'll stop us before you run into anything. He chuckled. Jamie seemed to enjoy his job.

After Jamie asked me to adjust the mirrors and showed me the location of the emergency brake, the turn signal, and the windshield wipers, I backed out of the driveway onto the street. The car was beginning to cool down slightly.

Let's go up here and turn left, he said. Nicholson it is, I think. Yup, Nicholson. He squinted at the street sign.

I turned on the windshield wiper instead of the turn signal and groaned.

Everyone does that when they're starting out, he said. Not to worry. We call that the "American wave." He snickered as he waved his arm back and forth.

Not my fault you guys put it on the wrong side.

Good on ya, Edie. Nice turn. Move to the right just a bit. Too much. Back a bit. There you go. Now we're just gonna follow this road.

You're doing great, he said. Much better than this lady from Texas I met last week. She was a nightmare. Her husband was a real tosser too. Oh, sorry, that's not too kind of me. He was from New York. You're not from New York, are you?

No, California.

Oh yeah? I been to California. Went to Universal Studios and Disney. Good stuff, California. Nice place.

I'm from San Francisco.

Ah, didn't get down there. Up there?

A cyclist was at my right front fender. I could feel myself sweating. Shit, I said.

You got some mouth on you, mate. You got this. Relax.

I exhaled as I passed her. She wasn't wearing a helmet. Sorry about the swearing, I said. I can't help it.

No worries, good to know I won't offend. All right, Edie, in a couple a blocks, you're approaching a roundabout. There's just one rule of roundabouts. Don't slow down. And yield to the right.

That's two rules.

Look to your right. That person's got the right of way. No one on your right? Keep going. The car on your left will wait for you.

Over the next hour, I drove in and out of more than twenty roundabouts and parallel parked seven times. We drove past the beach, past the billboard with the half man, half chess piece, and through Kings Park and ended up at Bunnings, an enormous home improvement store, where Jamie had me pull in and out of tight parking spaces. I felt like a remote control car, back and forth.

I'm just gonna run in, Jamie said. Stretch your legs if you like.

I took off my sunglasses and rubbed my eyes. I couldn't decide whether this driving lesson was a good idea. Jamie talked a lot. A man walked behind the car pushing a cart filled with PVC piping of various sizes and a potted lemon tree. He had a toddler with him, sitting in the front of the cart, eating a banana. She coughed and, for a moment, I thought she was choking.

I could have broken Dad's jaw.

I shuddered.

Jamie came back with a small bag and two hot dogs. Your first Bunnings sausage, he announced. It's a tradition. Cheers. He clunked his sausage against mine and laughed.

You'll get used to the weather, he said. Besides, sausage and a beer is good in any weather. He raised a cautionary finger. Of course, no beer when you're driving. He paused for a moment and said, So, Edie Richter, what are you gonna do in Perth? How will you busy yourself? With no little ones to look after.

Wiping the corner of my mouth with the paper napkin, I spoke quietly. I haven't really thought about it. We moved here quickly. We were dealing with some family stuff...My voice trailed off.

What was it you did back in San Fran?

I explained I worked in marketing for nonprofit organizations.

Just heard about this place that teaches kids how to grow beans and tomatoes and whatnot, Jamie said. I'll find out the name of it. I'll ask Bronnie. Bronnie's my daughter. She lives up north, but she's got more friends than any of us. She's about your age.

Thirty-eight?

He shrugged. Close. She'll be twenty-eight in June. Twenty-eight on the twenty-eighth.

I didn't want to talk anymore. I wiped my hands on my shorts and started the engine.

On the way home, Jamie asked me to pull into an alley off Selby Road. A sign said SPINE AND LIMB FOUNDATION OP SHOP. He said, pointing, Let's go in and you can choose something for that empty house of yours.

Jamie was certainly taking me on as his personal project, that was clear. I wondered if this was considered normal in Australia, if this was welcoming or nosy. But my house was empty, he was right about that.

I didn't want to spend too much time browsing, so I quickly purchased a small watercolor of a magpie in a wooden frame for twenty dollars. The lady wrapped it in tissue paper, and Jamie hung it for me in the living room, after he had fixed the screen door. Turns out his small bag from Bunnings was filled with nails, screws, and a mini-hammer.

Thank you, I said to him as he guzzled a glass of water in the kitchen. I mean besides just the driving obviously. I mean fixing the door, hanging the picture. That was really nice of you.

A baby cried.

Too easy, he responded. I noticed the logo on his shirt was actually meant to be a steering wheel, not a sun.

After Jamie left, I made an antioxidant smoothie with bananas and chia seeds and walked to the living room to sit in the air-conditioning. I felt tired. I wasn't used to talking to someone nonstop. Resting my glass on my knee, I closed my eyes and pictured a world map, the kind you might see on a classroom wall. I imagined a pea-sized version of me, standing in Western Australia, holding a piece of rope that stretched all the way to Sydney and then across the Pacific Ocean all the way to San Francisco. The rope was pulled tight and I felt it burn against my palm. I saw all the brown and green colors of the Australian states and a sliver of the blue ocean in the distance.

When I opened my eyes, I was looking directly at the magpie hanging on the wall. A bird alone on a grassy field next to a tree, head raised in surprise. He seemed to be looking right at me. What? I said to the bird. What do you know?

10

I read that oats have more soluble fiber than any other grain and that fiber reduces the absorption of cholesterol into your bloodstream.

I started soaking Bircher muesli in almond milk before bed. One morning I peeled off the plastic wrap, added chopped apple and almonds, and ate it standing up in the kitchen. A crow was perched on the fence outside, near the lemon tree. It spread its wings and looked like it was about to fly, but then jumped a few inches forward and lowered its wings. This seemed like a lot of effort for such a small gesture. I pulled on my blue-and-white-striped swimsuit and lightweight denim sundress, packed a bag, and drove to Cottesloe Beach, cursing when I passed a cyclist or went through a roundabout.

At a red light, next to a Red Rooster drive-through, I saw another billboard for the half man, half chess piece. This time I noticed it was an advertisement for TopRate Realty. VINCENT GUERRA, #1 IN SALES SINCE 2008. The man's eyes were looking directly at me. The light flashed green and the GPS told me I'd be turning right in five hundred meters. I flipped on the windshield wipers instead of the turn signal. Then I tuned the radio to a station where the DJs were regular people who played whatever they wanted. An enormous school campus passed by on the right, with a fancy metal gate and a sign that said BUILDING GOOD MEN. I pictured a factory that made giant dolls in pleated khakis and sensible shoes.

After a quiet song with lots of guitar strumming, a young man's voice came on the radio and said, *That was Holly Throsby and now, at the risk of sounding like a bit of a tosser, I'm going to play a twenty-three-minute track. This is "Pegasus" by the Wayne Shorter Quartet.*

I turned it up to hear the piano. A few minutes in, the song got loud and reminded me of a James Bond soundtrack. Then it quieted down again. I felt like I was chasing a dog through a forest.

Oren and I once drove from Boston to New York to go to a jazz club. It was a surprise for my birthday. In the middle of the show, my cell phone rang and everyone in the club, including Oren and the stand-up bass player with the curly mustache, glared at me. After the show, I stepped out to listen to the voice mail. It was Dad, wanting to know why I was late meeting him and whether we were supposed to be meeting. At the end of the message he whispered, I think your mother wants to kill me.

Now, heading west on Eric Street from Stirling Highway, I reached the top of a hill and inhaled sharply. The Indian Ocean was in front of me, bright blue and endless. Four cargo ships guarded the horizon. I parked next to a sign advertising SCULPTURE BY THE SEA. A rock jetty protruded from the shore like a giant's index finger.

I laid out my orange Coral beach towel and then promptly flipped it over to hide the logo. Entering the water, I immediately dove over a small wave and pushed my hands into the soft sand. I came up shivering but knew this would pass, because the water was much warmer than the Pacific. A school of translucent gray fish swam toward a bed of seaweed. Through the sting of the salt water, I stared at them until my eyes adjusted. I swam deeper and rotated onto my back to watch the sun from under the surface. My thoughts, like the waves, were there one minute and gone the next. *Where is that plane going? Should Oren and I see a movie tonight? Was that a rock? Why do people care about arts education?* Dad used to close his eyes at the symphony. He'd squeeze my knee once and pat it twice. Code for: *This is a beautiful song.* I curled my knees up to my chest and rolled over.

I swam farther out and could see a thin slice of land in the distance. Rottnest Island was named after the quokka, a squirrel-like animal that resides there. When Dutch settlers first saw quokkas, they thought they looked like rats. Rats' Nest. I learned this from Abby. I wondered what time it was in San Francisco.

Suddenly my left arm felt as if it had been dunked into a vat of ice water. This momentary chill morphed into a shooting pain. I spun around a couple of times, egg-beating my legs, but I didn't see anything other than a few pieces of seaweed. I bent my elbow and tried to examine my forearm, but the water was bumpy. My armpit felt like it was hovering over a lit match. I swam back to shore awkwardly and flopped on the sand, my left arm burning now. Tears swam from the inside of my nose to my eye sockets. The pain felt like razor burn and lemon juice and paper cuts and bee stings.

The sun beat down on my back. Everything in the world was hot. I clutched my arm to my chest as if I were protesting. I tried to slow down my breath. The heavyset woman used to talk about directing your breath to specific areas of your body. Including your heart, she had said. It helps with heartbreak. I tried to breathe into my arm, but I wasn't even sure what that meant. I blew from the inside of my elbow to my wrist repeatedly, as if it were covered in birthday candles. I dug my heels into the wet sand and rocked back and forth. Abby had warned me about the pervasiveness of jellyfish on the Perth coast. *Keep vinegar in your car*, Abby had written in a follow-up email, *it soothes the sting*. There was no vinegar in the car. The closest person was at least fifty yards away, a man in the water up to his waist.

Abby had also said to urinate on a jellyfish sting. Just as I wondered whether I could contort my body to squat over my arm, the pain started to change, moving from shooting to throbbing, and pink lines appeared on my arm like discarded pieces of string. I was not going to pee on my arm. I could make it back to the car.

With the motor and air conditioner running, I texted Oren. *Stung by jellyfish*. I looked for a jellyfish emoji but couldn't find one, so instead I sent a red octopus. On the radio, the casual DJ announced, *Here's Seu Jorge with "Bola de Meia." That translates to "sock-filled ball."*

I drove home, past Red Rooster, past the good man factory, and past VINCENT GUERRA, #1 IN SALES SINCE 2008.

11

Dad had a scar on his forearm, in the same location as my jellyfish sting. He was bitten by a rottweiler when he was a child but insisted he'd brought it on himself. He tried to pull a tennis ball out of its mouth, and the dog dropped the ball and latched on to Dad's arm.

Dad loved dogs. Mom wouldn't let him have one. It's like having another child, Paul. He made a point to introduce himself to every dog he passed on the street.

Does she shake hands? he once asked the owner of a shih tzu. I was home visiting from college and he and I were walking to the pharmacy.

The owner shook her head and laughed. Stella's not that smart.

Dad looked down at the dog. Yes, you are. Don't listen to her. He crouched down beside the small brown-and-white creature and held one of her front paws. I'm Paul, nice to meet you, Stella.

The owner and I stayed silent until Dad finished talking with the dog. It was a foggy day and my glasses were wet.

Shih tzus don't obey well, but they are quite smart, Dad said when we started walking again. In fact, refusing to obey can be a sign of intelligence, wouldn't you agree, Edie? He liked teasing me.

On Father's Day one year, Abby and I gave him a dog encyclopedia. He pored over the heavy book, sticking Post-its on his favorite breeds. Bavarian mountain hound, Carpathian shepherd dog, Norwich terrier. He'd bring up dog breeds in conversations about people. She sounds like a cross between a basset hound and a Parson Russell, he'd say about a girl in Abby's dance class. The problem is, he knows he's good-looking, he said about my soccer player boyfriend, just like a Rhodesian ridgeback. It drove Mom nuts.

Late into his illness, his hallucinations often had something to do with dogs. He would pat at an imaginary animal beside him or hold up his hand, as if offering it to a wet nose. He'd smile and say things like, Aren't you a pretty puppy.

Sometimes they terrified him. Invisible packs would gallop past his bed and he'd scream, Too close! Get back!

What is it, Dad? I'd ask, hopping up from a chair in the corner where I'd been reading. What's wrong?

The dogs, the dogs! he'd shriek, covering his eyes.

I'd say, There are no dogs here, Dad, you're safe, you're imagining this. This never seemed to help.

One day when I was clipping his toenails, he kicked me hard in the chest. No, no, no, no! he yelled. Get away from me!

Is it the dogs? I asked him.

He nodded vehemently and started crying. They're going to kill me, he said.

I put the clippers back on the cart and asked him, Where are they, Dad? Show me.

He pointed at the far wall, above the bookshelf.

I stomped over to the wall and screamed, Get out!

I looked back at Dad, who was now staring at me, mouth open slightly. I continued to yell at the wall. Get out! Leave him alone!

I waited a moment, then turned to Dad and said, I think they're gone. He nodded slowly. Can I finish cutting your nails now?

He smiled and said, Thank you, ma'am. I would like that very much.

12

Before I met my next-door neighbor in Perth, I saw her dancing in her living room. I was taking out the trash just as the sun was setting, the darkening sky streaked with orange. Spinning in circles with her baby, first one way then the other. The baby looked like he was laughing as his mom's blond braids whipped the sides of his face. As she slowed down, she held her baby up like a sacrifice, ankles in one hand, neck cradled in the other. Then she pulled him into her and kissed his stomach. She looked like an antidepressant commercial.

The next day, there was a knock at the door. Four taps. She was wearing a sleeveless white sundress and small gold hoop earrings. Her name was Fiona and she apologized for any screaming I may have overheard since moving in.

This little bloke is loud, she explained, glancing at the baby staring at me from his mother's hip. You have children?

No, I replied perhaps a bit too quickly.

She thought about this for a moment. Canadian?

No, San Francisco.

I've always wanted to go to San Fran. The baby squealed. He needs a sleep. I wanted to invite you next door for tea. Are you free now?

I—I'll be right over, I stammered. Just have to finish something.

Her house smelled of mildew and paint. Framed photos were crammed together on the top of the bookshelf near the front door. One metal frame had a thin layer of dust—a BEST FRIENDS plaque featuring five indistinguishable blondes holding champagne flutes. One photo was of an empty beach chair at a shoreline. Where's this? I asked her.

She laughed. That's my goal. That's what I tell Benny.

Your husband?

Bingo, she said.

I tripped on the rug leading down to the kitchen.

Fiona was a talker. She had a bright blue electric kettle and a large fish tank. The fish were not my idea, she said. Hopefully they don't eat each other.

I bent over and peered through the foggy glass. I only see two. Are there more?

Just those two, she said, pointing. Jane and Mr. Darcy.

She asked why we would leave San Francisco for Perth. When I told her Oren worked for Coral, she said Benny was also in mining. I told her I wasn't used to someone else working for an oil company, and she laughed. This is Perth, she said, I reckon it's quite common.

Fiona was from Melbourne, pronounced *Mel-bin*, and moved to Perth because Benny didn't try harder to get something in Melbourne. His family is here as well, not that they see the grandkids so that's no help. They're gray nomads.

Gray nomads?

His dad bought a camper and the two of them cruise around on a bit of a walkabout, I reckon.

I spotted a trampoline in the backyard. Do you jump with him? I asked, looking at the baby, who I thought was napping.

She laughed. No, that's for Livvie.

There's another one?

You haven't heard her? She's six and full of herself at the moment. Cheeky, that one. In year one. Borrow her any time. She pulled a school photo out of a pile of papers next to the fish tank and handed it to me. Brown pigtails and wide-spaced eyes. Livvie looked like a girl who always got told she looked like her father.

She looks nothing like the rest of us, Fiona said, seemingly reading my mind. We don't know where she came from.

Dad used to tell me he didn't know where I came from. You're a beautiful enigma, he said once after I spent one Sunday gathering up dust balls in the living room and presenting them to him in a Ziploc bag. He gave me a dollar and I ran to my room and pulled my big dictionary out from under the bed. *Enigma. A person or thing that is mysterious, puzzling, and difficult to understand.*

Years later, in a high school English class, I submitted a short essay with each sentence on a separate page. It was a story about a married couple in the process of divorcing. The teacher gave me a B and wrote on the cover of my booklet, *Edie, you are an enigma.*

Now, Fiona was making a pot of tea and talking about the man who used to live in our house. I was sitting at her kitchen table, which was covered in crumbs.

Livvie had told the man how much she loved Mickey Mouse, Fiona said, and then, a week later, on our veranda was an IGA bag filled with Mickey Mouse paraphernalia. A few t-shirts, a hat with ears, two DVDs, a tea towel. It was way too much, you know? It's bizarre to give a bag of toys to a six-year-old child you barely know. So that was the first clue.

She poured the tea into two small mugs that looked like they would be suitable for a baby shower, one light pink and one light blue.

She handed me the blue one and said, And his shoes were always perfectly shined. Not a scratch. It reminded me of when I was in St. Kilda, interviewing flatmates. My aunt told me to look at their feet, that if they take good care of their shoes, they'll take good care of the house. I ended up getting this gay bloke, gorgeous, wanted to be a stage actor, worked at a café where the waiters sing. He was a good roommate. He moved to America—I think he became a regular on one of those American murder shows. Where was I?

Fiona paused and stared at the table.

The man who used to live next door, I said. His shoes.

Oh, right. So this bloke's shoes were always sparkling and made of really fancy leather. He had this white pair that he wore with a white suit. White, head to toe, made his skin look orangey in that Italian way. Have you been to Italy? she said, her eyes squinting.

Once during college, I said. I went to visit a friend in Florence. She was doing a year abroad.

I didn't add that this friend had called me in a panic because she was pregnant as a result of a one-night stand with an apprentice butcher. Not even a real butcher, she had said in disgust. She couldn't bear to come home, so I flew there for a week. We managed to find a doctor who would perform an abortion while I did Sudoku in the waiting room.

Never been to Italy myself, Fiona said. But you know what I mean, that tanned troublesome look. And in a white suit, you can imagine.

He was attractive but not in the right way, like his head wasn't on straight.

She paused and tilted her head, listening for something. Was that Thomas? she said. He desperately needs a lie-down after last night's spectacle. She sipped her tea and redid her ponytail.

There were always people coming and going, she said. Stand up for a sec, come here. See that path? That goes to your side door. See?

Yes, I said.

So you know what I'm saying, she said. Every day, people in and out. Oh, sorry, sit down, I don't want your tea to get cold. Do you take sugar? I didn't offer you sugar.

No thanks, I said. I'll take honey if you have any.

She walked over to the pantry, pulled out a drawer that was stuffed with bottles and cans, and proceeded to announce its contents. Vanilla, jelly, tomato sauce. Sorry, Edie, no honey. Edith, sorry. Anyone call you Edie?

Most people call me Edie, actually.

She nodded and said, Where was I? Oh yes. So after dropping Livvie at school and doing whatever, I'd usually come home by ten to putter around and watch *Table Talk*. I was pregnant with Thomas. This was last year, really sick for months. Now you can see, when I was sitting on the couch watching TV, I could see the path and it was always busy. Sometimes another fancy bloke in shiny shoes would walk up, sometimes a bunch of them. Or a few girls too dressed for daytime. You know what I mean?

Was it loud? I asked her, sipping my unsweetened and slightly bitter tea.

The women?

No, I just mean the house in general, I said. Like, was there a lot of noise coming from there? Especially with all of the people coming and going?

You'd think so but no, not really. I mean, he had the occasional party. He'd always tell us beforehand. He'd say, I'm having a barbecue this weekend, it's my brother's birthday. Or niece's communion or something like that. But I never saw any children over there. Not once. And then we'd hear music but it never went too late, and the next day we'd always have something on our veranda like a few bottles of wine from Margaret River, or a gift basket with brie and biscuits. He was a good neighbor. Clearly up to something, but a good neighbor. Very polite. That's what I told the police when they came for him. I told them, Look, I don't know anything, but I can tell you he's probably the loveliest neighbor I ever had.

Did you see him get arrested?

Her eyes widened and she said, I saw them pull up, sirens and everything, and storm in there like he was a terrorist or something. It seemed dramatic. I mean, he wasn't going to put up a fight. There was no escape. They took him out in handcuffs, wearing that white suit in fact. He caught my eye through the window. I felt bad about that, felt bad that I was watching.

Did you ever see him again?

Just in the news reports. A few months later, I was at King Edward Hospital after having Thomas, and I received a Mickey Mouse balloon and the largest bouquet of yellow roses. Close to a hundred. Made the room smell absolutely fantastic.

She almost sang the last two words. *Absolutely fantastic.*

He was a nice man. She blushed slightly, remembering her neighbor.

*

That night I told Oren that a gangster used to live in our house.

You're pretty gangster, he said, snuggling into my shoulder.

No, I'm serious, I said, stroking his hair. A Perth gangster. Drugs and everything.

Just then, something scurried across the roof. It startled us. At the sound of clawing and groaning in the wall, Oren kissed my neck and said it sounded like mating time. I elbowed him and said, You can trap animals in your house but then you have to let them go. It's illegal to kill them.

Did you learn this from the cheerleader? Oren said, resting his hand on my stomach.

I stretched my arms over my head. I can't decide if I like her or not, I said.

He touched my nose and whispered, You say that about everyone, Edie.

I dreamed about Dad. He and I were walking on Cottesloe Beach. There were eucalyptus trees on the shoreline and, perched on the branches, possums with big black pupils. We had to walk between tall buildings protruding out of the sand. He held my arm and told me he pretended to die because he knew that's what I wanted. I told him I wasn't sure now. He told me to push one of the buildings over. Make it fall on me, Edie, he said. I refused and he grasped my arm tighter. Push it over, Edie. Do it, he growled. I woke up to the sound of hissing and screeching. It sounded like an attack. Oren twitched for a moment but remained asleep. I stared at the ceiling in horror.

My body was a collection of muscles and bones and a thing I had done.

My arm was asleep. I bit my flesh, halfway between my elbow and my wrist, not to break the skin, just to leave a mark.

13

It was hot and I went for a walk in Kings Park. I didn't bring a water bottle and spent several minutes slurping from the fountain at a playground named after an electric power company. I rested on top of the giant crocodile statue in the shade and watched a mother walk in circles with a stroller, trying to get her baby to fall asleep. Every so often she peeked over the top, sighed, then resumed walking. She caught my eye and gave me a raised eyebrow, like, Babies, right? I nodded back at her as if to say, I know, right?

I slept soundly as a child. I had a small white box on my nightstand that projected stars on the walls and ceiling, and when Dad said good night, he'd plug it in before turning off the big light. Look at all the stars, Edie, he'd say. You're inside but you're outside.

There were eighty-three stars altogether, until one night there were eighty-two. I called for Dad and told him that one of the stars was gone. He fiddled with the box and asked me to recount. Still eighty-two. Dad explained that real stars die sometimes, and how the death of one star can trigger the formation of new stars. He said there might be new stars now that I just couldn't see.

I left the park and came home to Fiona walking down my steps, long hair gathered on one side, baby on her hip. Her legs looked muscular and her toenails were painted fuchsia. She walked like someone who had been popular in high school. Dad once said what scared him most in movies were the mothers who made everything look effortless. I was really thirsty.

There you are! Fiona said, smiling. I saw your car so I thought you might be home. Good walk?

The baby was pulling on one of her small gold hoop earrings. I reached out and touched his bare foot. He pulled it away and nestled into his mother's clavicle, which stuck out like a railing above her lightweight pink t-shirt.

Hey, she said. We're going to Rottnest next week and I'm wondering if you'd feed the fish, bring in the bins, that sort of thing. Kate usually does it—she gestured across the street—but she's in the UK.

Sure, that's fine, I said, removing my sunglasses and wiping the sweat from my nose. I was thirsty.

She held the baby's wrist as he squirmed. You sure it's not a bother? she said.

No, it's fine, really, I said. I started walking up the stairs. I really needed some water.

Thanks, Edie. I'll get you the key. We leave Sunday. Back the following Sunday, she said, standing at the foot of my stairs, perhaps wanting to be invited in. She probably kept a gratitude journal.

I waved and went inside. I turned on the air-conditioning and drank water while watching a clip of a talk-show host interviewing a famous actress. The host was wearing a suit. His male sidekick was also wearing a suit. The famous actress was wearing shiny shorts, a shiny tank top, and high heels. The show was taped in New York City in February. She must have been freezing.

Fiona came back the next day with the key hanging from a key chain with a glittery *F*. And the day after that with a reminder about the mailbox. On Sunday, I stood and watched from the living room window as Fiona and her husband packed the car, argued about a beach tent, buckled the kids in, and eventually drove away.

After Oren left for work Monday morning, I went next door with the key. On the bookshelf, in front of the BEST FRIENDS frame, was a note:

Dear Edie,
The food is next to the tank. They get one pinch in the morning
and one again at night. If you forget one day, they won't die.
Ta!
Fi

Jane was hiding inside a rocky castle, and Mr. Darcy was nibbling at
the surface. After dropping in a few tiny colorful flakes, I pulled up a
kitchen stool and watched them for a while. Jane swam out from under
the castle's arch to find the food. She was orange with black spots, and
her back fin was large and translucent. Mr. Darcy was white with a
green-tipped top fin. He ignored Jane as he tried to suck in as much
of the food as possible. The tank was set up in front of a window that
faced the backyard. I wondered if the fish could see beyond the tank,
to the green grass and the trampoline. Like humans looking at the
ocean.

Staring at the tank made me thirsty. I opened the fridge, but all that
was in there was a bottle of sauvignon blanc, four beers, cheese, jam,
mustard, and a plastic container of purple rubbery goo. As I sipped
tap water from a glass engraved with a four-leaf clover, I stared out
the window to my own house and thought about what it would be like
to have a baby perched on my hip. I tried standing with more weight
first on one leg and then the other. I raised my hands above my head
and spun around.

I examined the bookshelves. British authors with pastel covers. A
scrawled drawing of an animal was in a red frame. On the bottom
right corner, someone, perhaps a teacher, had written, *Livvie says wom-*
bats make me feel tickly. I opened the frame to see if there were more
drawings underneath. There were not.

There was a book about tidying up, which I skimmed. The author said
to start with your clothes. Pull everything off hangers, out of drawers,
off the floor if needed, and pile it into a mountain. Then, holding one
item at a time in front of you, ask yourself whether it sparks joy.

I went through a pile of paper on the coffee table. A couple of school notices, a shiny brochure for a politician—*Peggy Taylor Listens and Gets Things Done*—take-out menus, a carpet cleaning service. Last week's Sunday newspaper was at the bottom of the pile. There on the lower half of the front page was *Vincent Guerra, #1 in Sales Since 2008*, except this time instead of half man, half chess piece, he had gardening shears for hands and stood in front of hedges that were in the shape of dollar signs. He had the same obnoxious smile. I turned over the paper and shoved it between the other junk.

I put my glass in the sink and went home.

14

The clothes hanging in my closet were arranged by color. The shoes, however, were in one large heap. It was a sign of something, I just wasn't sure what.

I lifted up a pair of black linen pants and examined them closely. The hanger had caused wrinkles at the knees and there was a small coffee stain near the side hem. These pants were very comfortable and matched everything, but I couldn't say whether they sparked joy.

In the kitchen, I poured myself a glass of kombucha and checked my email. There was a note from an environmental organization in Marin County. It was launching a program where staff drove inner-city kids out to watershed restoration projects and had them clean up while learning about nature. This was not how Martin from marketing described the program, but that was the gist of it. Would I be willing to craft the fund-raising messaging around this initiative, and how much did I cost and what would be the timeline? Martin knew that I was living in Perth—What is *that* like?—and he knew it might be a while before he heard back from me because of the time difference. I wrote back with my hourly rate and an anecdote about petting a kangaroo at a local wildlife park.

Oren texted about buying a lightbulb for his reading light only if I was heading out, it wasn't urgent.

I ate an apple and watched a magpie fly back and forth from our roof to the neighbors' fence, repeating this dance over and over. When it landed on the fence, it paced a few times, lifting its feet to some imaginary beat and placing them down carefully as if wearing swim fins. The whole routine—roof to fence, pacing, and back to roof—took between thirty-five and forty seconds.

Dad took me to a Philip Glass opera when I was in high school. It had a Civil War theme, and the melody repeated over and over like a firing squad. Your mother didn't want to go, he had said. Philip Glass makes her want to jump off a bridge. I wish he hadn't told me this, because knowing my mother hated his music made me want to feel about Philip Glass the way I felt about swimming, immersed and safe, but one minute into the overture, I hated the music with a rage I couldn't hide. These seats were expensive, Dad said at intermission. We're not leaving early.

I spent the second act staring at a woman's shiny shoulder blades. Driving home, Dad didn't say a word.

I returned to the pile of clothes on my bed and held up a faded green t-shirt that I bought at a used-clothing store a few years ago. It used to have a tiny yellow stripe across the bottom but that was gone now. I threw the t-shirt, along with an unworn red blazer, into a plastic bag and hung everything else back up in my closet.

I retraced the drive I did with Jamie and found the enormous hardware store. I bought an assortment of lightbulbs because I had forgotten to bring along the broken one. I also bought a plastic tub for storing the lightbulbs and a metal shoe rack.

The thrift shop had a sign in the window that said NOW ACCEPTING DONATIONS OF CLOTHING AND BOOKS. After I handed the bag over to the smiling young man with glasses and Down syndrome, I walked to the back of the store, past the plastic toys and kitchenware, to a hand-written sign that said SUNDRESSES AND WOMEN'S SKIRTS. It had started raining and I was in no hurry to get back. Running my hand across the rack, the fabrics were mostly very soft, with the occasional stiff denim. I bought a black linen sundress with small red buttons down the front.

Later that night, after feeding the fish, I tried on my new used sundress. Oren looked up from his laptop and said I looked feminine and did I want to watch something? Sitting on the couch in front of a show about the near future where technology has become even more frightening, we ate tofu curry with turmeric and rice noodles.

I discovered a grocery list in the pocket of the sundress. *Milk, eggs, muesli, pasta, garlic, capsicum, toms.* On the bottom right corner was a phone number and the letters *ASA*. I tucked the paper between the pages of a library book, *Walking Trails of Perth*, and looked over at Oren, who was fast asleep.

I remembered the dinner conversation the night after the Philip Glass opera.

I told you she wouldn't like it, Paul.

Does that make you happy, Louise?

I haven't been happy in years, Paul.

For the love of god, Louise, that's not my problem.

Abby was little and watched them bicker back and forth like a game of ping-pong.

I stood up and slammed both hands on the table. Stop it! I yelled. Fucking stop it!

My parents turned their heads and looked at me with stone faces.

Philip Glass is an idiot, I said. You're both fucking idiots.

Abby started crying. I pulled her out of her highchair and carried her upstairs. I could hear Mom and Dad starting up again. Forget them, I said to Abby as I tucked her fairy comforter under her chin, you don't belong to them. I lay down next to her and she nestled against me. A tiny spark of joy.

15

It started raining when I was on the phone with Mom. We needed to choose a headstone for Dad and she knew it wasn't a fun conversation but it was important. Edie, your sister is not being helpful.

Lightning crashed at 9:41 A.M. Mom heard it through the phone. Edie, can you go in another room? I can't hear you.

No, Mom, I can't. It's lightning.

We decided on DEVOTED HUSBAND, FATHER, AND FRIEND. Mom thought *Father* should come first, but I told her she knew him for longer.

I brought my book next door. Mr. Darcy was pecking at the side of the tank when I arrived and swam quickly to the surface to suck up the flakes. He seemed to have a preference for the red ones. Jane was hiding in the castle. You'd better hurry, I told her. Your roommate is on a rampage.

I walked down the hall to the girl's room. The door was closed and covered in butterfly and smiley-face stickers. The room was pink and smelled like a basement. Labeled plastic tubs lined the back wall. LEGOS, ELECTRIC TOYS, BLOCKS, DOLL CLOTHES. I pulled a small toy rabbit and a small toy cat out of the box marked SYLVANIANS. They were both wearing tiny human clothes. I buttoned the cat's jacket before returning it to the bin. A book about a tree house was at the foot of the bed.

I found some lavender lotion in the bathroom and applied it to my hands and ankles. I made a long black coffee with the espresso machine that used plastic pods and tripped on the corner of the rug. My coffee spilled all over the cream-colored rug.

Shit.

I swung open kitchen cupboards and searched for stain remover. Unlike the books and DVDs, there seemed to be a complete lack of organization when it came to the contents of the kitchen. Next to a box of Weet-Bix, I found baking soda and shook it over the stain. There was something called Ecover Natural Stain Remover on a shelf next to the dishwasher that I sprayed on top of the baking soda. I crouched down next to the stain.

Shit. It was bad.

I hopped up and grabbed the bottle of dishwashing liquid from the windowsill and squirted that on the stain. I tore several paper towels from the roll, laid them one by one over the wet mess, and pressed down hard with the heel of my hand.

I don't know what I was expecting. This was a mess. I repeated the steps. Baking soda, Ecover spray, dishwashing liquid. Nothing. I looked over at the fish tank. Mr. Darcy was sucking algae off one of the corners.

After a few minutes of staring at the pile of wet paper towels, I remembered the stack of papers and found the brochure for the carpet cleaning service. I called and they had an opening the next morning. They were offering a special where if you got two rugs cleaned, they'd do the couches for free. Sure, why not.

The rain had cleared, so I went out back with a glass of water and my book, *Walking Trails of Perth*. I leaned back on the lounge chair under the awning and opened to a section on East Perth. The grocery list fell on my lap. *ASA* and the phone number. I don't know why but I pulled out my phone.

Alzheimer's Support Australia, how may I help you?

I hung up and tossed my phone on the grass.

A few minutes later, I called again from Fiona's landline.

Alzheimer's Support Australia, how may I help you?

Yes, hello.

Hello, may I help you?

I don't know.

Are you experiencing memory loss?

No.

Is someone in your family having problems with their memory?

Yes.

From the looks of it, you're calling from WA?

Yes, I am in Perth.

We have support groups in Perth if you are interested. They are specifically for family members. A place to discuss common issues, talk to people who understand what you're going through. Free of charge, just a gold coin donation if you are able. Where are you in Perth exactly?

Subiaco.

Let me look that up. Sorry, the computer's being slow. There's a group at the community center, you know where that is?

Yes.

It's on Thursday fortnights. Tomorrow is the next one. From four to five. Craig is the bloke who leads it. Says here he's a licensed social worker.

I told Oren about the Alzheimer's meeting, which seemed to please him. I did not tell him about the spill. This might have complicated our relationship with the new neighbors.

The next morning, I was at Fiona's early to meet the cleaners. The stain had faded slightly from yesterday, but it was still noticeable.

Two men got out of a truck with the tagline A CLEAN LIFE IS A HAPPY LIFE, and I led them into the house. They looked at the rug, and one of them told me a long story about cat urine. This is nothing, they said. Piece of cake. I showed them the rug in the girl's room, the two couches in the living room, and the micro-suede love seat near the kitchen. Easy, they said. We'll be in and out in less than two hours. No, I wouldn't mind if they parked in my driveway. They meant Fiona's driveway of course. They came in with hoses and blue disposable shoe covers, an extra pair for me.

By eleven, the stain was gone and I was to use the paper shoe covers for the next twenty-four hours. I fed the fish and went home.

16

My parents sat me down soon after I got my period and told me boys only think about sex and to be careful. This is what my mother said anyway, and she followed it up with Right, Paul? My father played with a string hanging off his shirt and said quietly, Louise, I don't think you can stereotype all males that way. She told him he wasn't helping, and then he made a joke, saying he only thought about sex after he got married. He squeezed her knee and kissed her on the cheek.

Soon after, I had a boyfriend who always wanted to have sex. I didn't want to. It's not that I was particularly interested in protecting my virginity, but I didn't want sex the way I didn't want eggplant or skiing. He pushed the idea constantly and was dissatisfied with simply making out. It wasn't fair, he'd say, the way I'd tease him. He'd stare at the bulge in his jeans and say, Look what you've done to me. He'd stick my hand down his pants and help me jerk him off until he came. I'd stare at the bookshelf or the doorknob, as my wrist began to ache and he squealed like a pig.

Finally, one night, after a school dance, we went back to his house to make out. He started up again, asking why I wouldn't have sex with him, showing me his stiff penis, telling me how good it would feel, about how much he needed it. I looked him in the eye and told him I was raped. It was a family friend, I said, no one he knows. It was a couple of years ago. The friend and I had been watching TV when he crawled on top of me, pinned me down, yanked up my skirt, and forced himself inside of me. I limped home and never told anyone until now. The lie tumbled out of me like a landslide. The details offered themselves as beautifully wrapped gifts that I tore open with ease. This is why I don't want to have sex with you. This is why I can't have sex with you.

My boyfriend cried. He felt awful. I'm so sorry, Edie, all those times I pressured you, if I had only known. Why didn't you tell me? You are brave for telling me. I promise to never ask you again. I love you.

He kept his promise. He never pressured me again. His girlfriend was a rape victim and he had been selfish. He drew an outline of his hand on a piece of lined paper and told me I'd never be alone. We dated for a few more months until he admitted, crying, that he had cheated on me with a girl on the tennis team. He said, crying, that he still really needed to have sex but he didn't want to beg me and he hoped I understood. I told him I was happy for him actually, that he finally got to put his penis inside of a vagina, because that is all he ever wanted. We both got what we wanted.

I ran into him years later at a party. He pulled me aside to tell me it was good to see me and how he still felt bad about what happened. What do you mean? I asked him.

You know, he said quietly, what happened to you.

I remembered that I had lied about being raped. Forget about it, I said. I'm fine. How are you?

We spoke awkwardly for a few minutes and then he walked off to get a drink.

17

The handwritten sign on the door to the community center said ALZHEIMER'S SUPPORT AUSTRALIA SUPPORT GROUP. Two *supports*.

You're nice and early, Craig said. Good on you. My mum used to say if you're on time you're late. Biscuit?

When he pointed at the paper plate piled with shortbread and chocolate cookies, I noticed his diamond pinkie ring. Craig did not look like a social worker, or at least in the way I was expecting. He was wearing jeans and work boots and a green collared shirt with the ASA logo. He looked too old to be named Craig and have a buzz cut, but I was in Australia so what did I know.

He asked if I lived nearby and if I was Canadian. We made small talk.

Once you said *blocks* I knew you were American. I've always enjoyed that. I live down the block, he said, attempting an American accent. Have a seat, we'll start when we get a few more people.

I took one shortbread and a paper napkin and sat on one of the folding chairs set up in a circle. Balancing the cookie on my knee, I checked my phone. Abby texted, *The more I think about it, I can't even.* I tried to remember what we had spoken about yesterday. I turned off my phone and slipped it into my backpack.

Two older men arrived together. They seemed comfortable, regulars I guessed. A woman walked in, about my age, her red cheeks spotted with acne, holding a tote bag that said UWA UPMARKET. Another woman with bad posture who walked carefully was accompanied by a young man in an oversized denim jacket.

Craig spoke to everyone before they sat down. Geraldine, no Anzac biscuits today, I'm afraid to tell you.

The woman with bad posture swatted Craig playfully on the arm. How dare you, she said, flirting. Her escort in denim said nothing and looked at the floor.

The room had dark brown carpet, black-and-white photographs of official-looking old people, and one large stained-glass panel depicting what looked like the Last Supper. Maybe this used to be a church.

This could have been a mistake.

Let's all go around and introduce ourselves, said Craig. We have someone new here today.

I'm Geraldine. My husband has Alzheimer's. This is my nephew Gerald. He was named after me.

Gerald removed his denim jacket and hung it on the back of his chair. I guess I don't need an introduction, he mumbled.

The two older men were brothers. Their mother had dementia. We're just trying to learn all we can.

Tote Bag had a name I couldn't pronounce and immediately forgot. Plus, she spoke quietly, which didn't help. A few others said their names and why they were here. I went last.

I'm Edie. I'm American. My father has Alzheimer's. I paused. Had Alzheimer's.

Did he pass? Craig asked. I nodded. I'm sorry, he said. Was it while you were living here? I shook my head. Well, it's good you came, Edie. Welcome. Just so you know, I usually bring some sort of topic to the group, and sometimes we talk about that and sometimes we don't. Right, Geraldine?

Or we talk about biscuits, said Geraldine.

Today I wanted to bring the word *identity* to all of you. This comes up in issues of disease, particularly a disease affecting memory. How does your loved one see themselves? How do you see yourself, as a carer? Or how did you see yourself? He gestured toward me. Does anything come up for anyone when I say the word *identity*?

Tote Bag said her father no longer recognized her and she started crying. Craig walked across the circle with a box of tissues. One of the brothers said their mother was a nurturer and this role reversal was difficult for everyone. Of course it is, said Craig. That is one of the most challenging aspects of dementia. Changing roles, having a certain amount of flexibility with your identity. You are now someone who has to care for someone in a way that perhaps you never thought you would.

Craig turned to me. Edie, how was this for you? How did your identify shift throughout the progression of your father's disease? He took a sip of coffee. You are still quite young. I imagine this must have been quite a bit for you to take on.

Geraldine looked at me and shook her head.

Craig added, Of course, you don't have to say anything at all. No forced sharing in my groups. He smiled.

I took a deep breath and said, I'm not sure. It's nothing I've really thought about.

That's ok, Craig said. We can come back to you.

I mean, I guess I've thought about it but never really focused on it.

Identity is a weird way of putting it.

Putting what?

I mean, we just don't really understand anything.

Very true, Edie. He clasped his hands on his lap and smiled. A beam of sunlight streaming in through the stained glass hit his pinkie ring. Tiny dots of light danced on the wall, under a photograph of a scowling man in a suit.

I kept talking. We see ourselves one way, or many ways in relation to different people, I guess. But our identity, like who we are, who we really are, no one knows this. Some people say they are a certain way, identify a certain way, but it's all kind of bullshit.

How so?

I mean, I guess I thought of myself as my father's daughter, but this wasn't exactly an identity, more of a fact. When he got sick, I was still his daughter. He was still my father I guess, but he didn't always think he was my father. Sometimes he thought I was a stranger, or his girlfriend, or a nurse, or someone from a long time ago. His identity shifted by the minute probably. Or my identity in relation to him. Whatever you want to call it.

The room had gone silent. Outside a crow sighed. I took a breath and continued speaking.

We just never really know who we are. People might say things like, You're the kind of person who does the right thing, or I could never do what you're doing. I mean, in terms of identity, they might try and label you as someone who cares, someone who would go to great lengths to help people. And then they'll say they wouldn't do the same. But maybe they would do the same, maybe there is just this one shared identity and we're all part of it. Maybe we don't have our own unique selves, there's no such thing as individual identities.

Craig nodded. It seems like you're talking about the notion of identity negotiation. Identity in terms of role-playing. I'm curious about your personal identity, Edie, how you see yourself apart from the different roles you play in your life. You said that people often tell you that you always know what to do.

I don't think I said that.

That you do the right thing. Do you feel pressure to do the right thing? Did you feel pressure to do right by your father?

My hands were trembling. I crossed my legs, tucking my hands in between my thighs.

I spoke quietly. At the beginning, yes. There were many decisions to make, like whether or not to keep him at home, when to give him morphine, when to stop force-feeding him. You never know if you're doing the right thing, so you just think about doing the easy thing.

What he would have wanted, you mean? Craig said.

No. What the rest of us wanted. How the rest of his life was going to happen. He stopped being himself and I guess we stopped being ourselves. I stopped being myself. He had disappeared completely in the end. It had taken everything out of him. I mean, I guess he was still my dad. But not really.

Of course he was your dad, Edie, Craig said. He'll always be your dad.

I suddenly felt very uncomfortable. I didn't know why I was sitting in this depressing community room with its ugly brown carpet and Jesus stained glass, talking about something I knew nothing about. I stood up and flung my backpack over my shoulder. Sorry, I think I should go. I need to go.

I walked home quickly, as if I were being followed. A flock of rainbow lorikeets flew overhead and landed on a eucalyptus tree outside the bakery. The sun beat down on the back of my neck and the tops of my feet, between the leather straps of my sandals. I avoided looking at Fiona's house and ran up the stairs. Standing in the shower, I remembered the way my father vibrated under the weight of my hand, the moment I ended one thing and started something else. This thought overwhelmed me, and I sat down on the wet tiles, my feet on either side of the drain. Red stripes crisscrossed the tops of my feet like bruising from a beating. A small spider was on the shower floor, stuck in a puddle near my big toe. I brushed it into my palm, cracked open the shower door, and released it onto the floor. It scurried to the wall.

My father's body had trembled. It had come to life just before it died. There could have been a small moment of recognition. He could have understood that this was his oldest daughter, Edie, sitting beside him, pushing against his face. This was unlikely, but he could have.

I didn't know who I was before, or after, or at the exact moment I covered my father's mouth and asked him to forgive me.

18

Oren and I went to see the American musician Sufjan Stevens perform at the Red Hill Auditorium, just northeast of Perth in the Swan Valley. We drove at dusk, with the windows down, the sun on one side and the moon on the other. Kangaroos hopped along the edge of the highway. Stay, Oren called out the window, and laughed. We had been warned of kangaroos wandering onto the road at this hour.

An open-air sandstone amphitheater, the stage was positioned below a semicircle of tiered seating. It was a still, warm night.

While Oren went to find seats, I stood in line for beer and fries. Chips. Balancing two plastic cups and a steaming paper cone, I wandered up and down the steep aisles looking for him. Couples were nestled together, sharing paella and nachos. Groups of girls in high-waisted jeans and sandals laughed loudly. A man with a beard and a pigtail smoked a joint, while his friend craned his neck to catch a glimpse of a girl in a halter top passing by.

I couldn't find him. I had forgotten what he was wearing. This surprised me, as I could name every shirt in Oren's wardrobe and could tell you when he last wore each one. Had he changed after work? He wouldn't attend a show in one of his pale blue office shirts. I took a sip from one of the beers. It was lukewarm and tasted like burned toast. The short-sleeved brown one? The soft red one? The black t-shirt he bought online that said HUG DEALER? A woman with denim shorts and bright blue hair walked past me, carrying a cardboard tray with four cups of white wine. SSB it was called here. Semillon sauvignon blanc.

I paused at the top of one of the aisles and put down the drinks on a high table near the bar. I ate a fry and checked my phone. *Lower left, I'll look for you.* I scanned the theater. There, in the middle of hundreds of strangers, in his soft red t-shirt, was Oren, standing up, looking at me, waving his arms. He was wearing his Fitbit.

I could see you the whole time, walking up and down the stairs, he said after I handed him one of the beers. I was wondering when you'd find me, he added, pulling me into him.

The theater lights dimmed as the sun disappeared behind the stage. Sufjan played something from his album *Illinois* and then spoke quietly into the microphone: It's good to be here. The end of the earth, the beginning of the universe.

I closed my eyes as the band launched into a new song involving a lot of syncopation.

My father's heartbeat slowed significantly in those last couple of months, which was normal for someone in his condition. The heavy-set woman showed me how to massage his hands with my thumbs and suggested I do this when I visited him. I said I'd rather not, but she insisted. Sometimes simple acts of affection can be very helpful, she said. She brought in a small amber bottle of lavender eucalyptus oil and placed it on his bedside table.

This became something I did. Every so often while massaging him, I would stop, press my thumb into his wrist, and feel for his pulse. It was faint, as if under a heavy blanket.

One day James Taylor was on the stereo and I pressed his wrist to the beat of "Carolina in My Mind." This action caused his fingers to jerk forward. It's just a reflex, the heavyset woman informed me, from the corner of the room where she was sitting in the leather chair, working on her embroidery.

It looks like he's pressing on piano keys, I said to her.

Was your father a musician? she asked.

He loved music but didn't play anything, I said, squeezing two more drops of oil on my palm. I massaged each of his fingers, beginning with the little one, and lightly snapped the tips like the woman had shown me. I rubbed the small webs between his fingers and turned his hand over to feel the blue veins poking up through his paper skin. The oil made the veins shiny and they looked like tiny strips of neon lighting.

His wrists and arms were pale and skinny. Pouches of wrinkled skin hung down off his elbows like tiny udders. His eyes were closed and his mouth hung open slightly as if in midsentence. I don't know if he can feel any of this, I said to the heavyset woman.

I like to think he can, she said, he just doesn't have the energy to let you know.

I knew she was trying to get me to talk. My silence made her uncomfortable, or at least that's what my mother had told me. She wants to get to know us, Mom had said, that's her job. I told Mom, She's not our travel agent. If anything, she's Dad's travel agent.

You can put your head on his chest if you like, it won't hurt him. You can feel his heart beating.

No thanks, I said, and then when she left the room to make a call, I scooted closer to Dad, pulled down his gray blanket, and leaned over to rest my head on his ribs. His chest felt delicate through the green-checked hospital scrubs, and he smelled like wet rocks. His heartbeat was steady but slow, and my head bobbed up and down rhythmically. I closed my eyes and felt like I was floating in a lake.

I must have stayed in that position for quite some time, because when I sat up, my back hurt. It's good you're here, Edie, the heavyset woman said quietly. I hadn't realized she had returned and felt like I had been caught.

I stammered, I—I want to say things to him, but I'm just not sure what.

She put down her sewing, walked over, and sat down next to me on Dad's bed. I've been with many people in this situation, Edie, many people like your father, she said, resting her hand on mine. Family members all say the same three things. Doesn't matter what kind of relationship they had. The same three things. She shook her head and smiled.

What are they?

I love you. I forgive you. Please forgive me.

I suddenly felt thirsty. Do you think he's thirsty? I asked her, dry swallowing. She patted my knee and stood up to get an ice cube to rub along his gums.

Now, people in the crowd were singing along to a song I didn't know. I sipped my beer and looked over at Oren. I reached over and lightly touched the stubble on his cheek. His face felt warm. He turned to me and smiled. This is amazing, he said. The end of the world. He put his arm around me.

We sat like that for a while and swayed gently to the beat. It was at that instant I realized there had been exactly two moments in my life when I was entirely where I wanted to be. One was the day I rested my head on my father's chest one week before I killed him, and one was right now, with Oren at an open-air concert in the hills of Western Australia. I looked over the top of the stage, into the darkness.

19

A text from Fiona. *We're home. Could I pop by?*

I didn't write back. I had just finished vacuuming and could still be vacuuming. A few minutes later, the doorbell rang. Her silver necklace looked like a highway intersection.

Sorry, I was vacuuming. Did you have a good trip?

Rotto was beautiful, thanks. She paused and looked at me as if I had something on my face. Did you have the carpets cleaned when we were gone?

I spilled coffee and couldn't get the stain out, I said.

That's ok, you shouldn't have worried about it. We spill things all the time. The house smells odd and Benny's worried about the kids and the fumes.

I'm sorry. I aired it out all day yesterday. It still smells?

You really didn't have to do that, Edie. She shook her head. I wish you wouldn't have.

It wasn't expensive. You had a coupon in the mail.

She looked irritated now. She had returned from an island vacation to a clean house and did not appreciate the trouble I went to. She probably played in the waves with her children.

I asked her whether they did any snorkeling on the island, but I don't think she wanted to talk anymore. She asked for the key and went home.

Later that night, I was dicing carrots for a stir-fry when my phone buzzed.

Did you reorganize the pantry?

Yes, I wrote back. *It's no big deal. I enjoy things like that.*

I didn't receive a response. I saw her the next day—we were both returning from errands—but she went inside without saying anything.

20

Two years ago, I was hired by a nonprofit in New York that sends autistic children to summer camp. They invited me to fly out from San Francisco to lead a workshop for their board of directors called "Communicating the Message."

On the flight, I sat next to a small woman with a large bag. She was in the window seat and had frizzy brown hair that she had tied back in a messy ponytail secured with a plain rubber band. She had clear glossy nail polish and extra rubber bands around her left wrist. She wore a starched button-down shirt and yoga pants, like her top and bottom disagreed on the level of formality required for an airplane voyage. The middle seat between us was empty, and after takeoff, the woman dumped a stack of folders on it. The folders were red, yellow, and green, and I wondered if the colors were selected based on the sense of urgency assigned to each project.

The woman ordered a can of Diet Coke (no cup), downed it within a few minutes, and pushed the call button to request another. She sipped the second one more slowly, as she reviewed the contents of one of the yellow folders. She wrote notes in the margins and did a lot of circling and crossing out.

After I finished my cup of orange juice, I began reviewing my slide deck.

She turned to me. I bet your work is more interesting than mine, she said.

I doubt it, I said, unless your job is counting the number of rats in the New York subway.

The woman burst out laughing and then wiped her nose with the small white napkin. Good point, she said, that would be an awful job, wouldn't it?

Yes, I said, it would be pretty bad.

What do you do? she asked, stretching out her clasped palms and cracking her knuckles.

I'm a fund-raising consultant, I said. More marketing, I corrected myself. How to talk about what you do so you get people to give money.

She gave this some thought. So like the San Francisco Symphony would hire you to figure out why people would donate to an orchestra?

Pretty much, I said.

That's interesting actually, she said. You win.

You look like you're working on something big. I gestured at the pile of folders.

I'm a private investigator, she said.

Do you spy on people?

The people who work for me do that. I do more of the planning and follow-up. But right now, I'm basically grading papers. Going over my team's notes, giving feedback. I hate giving feedback. I mean, formally, in this way. She lifted up the yellow folder on her fold-out tray and made a disgusted face, tongue sticking out.

I don't know, I said. Even saying you're a private investigator sounds cooler than consultant.

Maybe I've just been saying it too long. Been in business for almost thirty years.

My eyebrows shot up. She was much older than she looked.

She reached into her bag and pulled out a small bottle of red nail polish. You mind? she asked. I shook my head.

She put the yellow folder back on top of the pile and clipped back her tray. Then she brought one of her bare feet up from the floor, rested her heel on the edge of the seat, and began painting her toenails bright red.

As she waved the paper vomit bag back and forth over her feet, she turned to me and said, The things we do. She meant we, as in women, but I had never once painted my toenails on or off an airplane and she didn't know that.

We do a lot of things, I said.

She asked many questions, not surprising for a private investigator. Where I grew up, where I went to college, how long I'd be in New York, why I left Boston for San Francisco, how long my dad had had Alzheimer's, his estimated time left. I didn't know how to answer this last question. It could be a while, I said. No one knows.

It's an awful disease, she said. Awful. You seem too young to have a parent with Alzheimer's.

That's what I thought, I said. I thought it was a grandparent's disease.

That's a good way of putting it, she said. It's a shitty grandparent's disease.

The flight attendant served us chicken with pasta and green beans, with a wilted fruit salad and shortbread cookie. We talked while we ate. Her name was Connie, she'd had breast cancer, but now she was better and divorced. No kids. She thought her job was too dangerous to bring kids into it. Turns out the cancer would have been worse, she said. Anyway, good decision either way.

Do you have any kids? she asked.

I shook my head. We decided not to, I said.

Take it from me, she said. Your whole life people will tell you that you made a mistake not having kids, but the minute something bad happens in the world or to you personally, they'll say thank god you don't have kids.

She took a bite of soggy cantaloupe and said, Do what you want with your life, Edie. It flies by.

We both watched the in-flight movie, a comedy about a family on a road trip, and then a television show about magic tricks and how our brains deceive us. As I wrapped the cord around my headset, Connie asked where I was staying in New York. Turns out my hotel was near her apartment and she offered to give me a lift.

Standing next to Connie in an airport rather than sitting beside her in the air was like seeing a teacher outside of the classroom. A man was waiting at baggage claim with a printed sign. This is Edie, she said to the man. We're going to drop her off at her hotel. When the driver smiled at me, I noticed his very white teeth.

As I stepped into the limousine, I wondered if perhaps I should have gotten a taxi instead. Connie sat across from me, scrolling through her phone. I looked out the window as we approached the New York skyline. It was rush hour, and the car lights sparkled.

I'm sorry, I need to make a call, Connie said suddenly, looking up from her phone. It's urgent.

That's fine, I said.

It's confidential, she said. She looked at me over her reading glasses. She looked different from this angle, not as small as she looked on the airplane.

That's fine, I repeated. I wasn't sure what she wanted. There was nowhere for me to go. I suggested I listen to music on my headphones if she wanted.

She looked relieved and put on her headset. Yes, thank you, that would be great. I'm sorry, it's just that it's private, she said.

A private investigation? I said, smiling at her. She didn't smile back, she was in a rush.

I got out my phone and earbuds and put on a blues album that Oren liked. Connie mouthed, *Thank you*. I nodded and resumed looking out the window.

After a minute or so, I turned down the music.

She was speaking in a voice that was low and angry. Just hold him until I get there, she was saying. Listen to me. Do not say a word. Do not say a single word to him.

I swallowed and stared at the highway barrier, trying to look like I was enjoying a song.

What sort of condition is he in? she said. What did they do to him?

In the reflection, I saw Connie lean forward and rest her arms on her thighs. She didn't say anything for a minute or so. And then she said, Listen to me. Do not repeat any of what you just said to anyone. He needs to pay for this. He needs to fucking pay for this. I'll be there as soon as I can. Making one quick stop.

She glanced at me in the window and saw that I was watching her. I averted my eyes and moved my shoulders back and forth slightly to the beat of the music I had turned down.

She was going to kill someone.

In a few minutes, she tapped my knee. *All done,* she mouthed.

I took out my earbuds and put them in the pocket of my backpack along with my phone.

Almost there, she said. She pointed out my window at a brick high-rise apartment building. I grew up near there, in the building behind that one.

I didn't say anything. I no longer believed her.

We pulled up outside of the hotel and the driver got my suitcase out of the trunk. Connie reached across and touched my knee. I am trusting you, she said, staring at me. She knew I had heard her.

Thank you for the ride, I said quietly, not looking back at her, and climbed out of the car as quickly as possible. As they drove off, I inhaled the freezing night air and held it in my lungs.

The next day I thought I saw her in the doorway of a mirrored office building.

Now, years later, across the world, I thought about this woman I met on a plane. It's not as if she placed my hand over my father's mouth. She didn't tell me to kill him. But I wondered if she somehow planted the seed.

This seemed like a stretch.

21

One night in Perth, I dreamed that I was lying on my back on a stage, feet pointing to the back curtain, my head dangling off the front. A large projector screen hung directly above my chin, and every time I exhaled, a small image appeared on the screen. At first, the images were nothing memorable, butterflies and sunflowers, like a teenager's tattoos. As my breath deepened and my exhales became longer, the pictures became gruesome. A giant hand holding a bloody knife, a puppy being force-fed, a woman being raped by a human-rhinoceros hybrid. When I screamed, the images turned even more horrific, so I had to keep quiet as they scrolled. When I woke up I felt like I had been dragged through hot lava.

The next morning, driving to Leederville, I tried pretending I didn't do it. I invented a story with lots of details about how I kissed his cheek, told him I loved him, then left the house and drove home. He died later that night, naturally. There was nothing noteworthy about his death. It was a run-of-the-mill ending. This could have easily happened. I could have made it all up.

In Leederville, I read the newspaper in a café with rock concert posters plastered all over the walls and giant paper lanterns hanging from the ceiling. I took a bite of a gluten-free muffin. Maybe I reorganized his drawers and that's why I took out the blue t-shirt. I could have been not in my right mind—my father was dying after all—and thought that refolding shirts might help me focus on something trivial and controllable.

I walked to a health food store and bought a ten-mushroom blend powder and ginger paste for an alkalizing tonic. I'd read it boosts metabolism.

I was alone with him when it happened. There were no witnesses.

This could be a story about a woman who thought so much about killing her father that she convinced herself she did it. The only way to prove her innocence would be to confess to a crime she didn't commit. What an ending.

I drove a longer way home to avoid a Vincent Guerra billboard where he was made to look like the Incredible Hulk.

On the way, I stopped at a grocery store called Angry Almond to pick up some medjool dates, high in carbohydrates. The man with the striped beanie and leather necklace asked me if there was anything else I needed. I had been staring into space. He asked me if I wanted to sample the vegan brownie and I said, No thank you, I killed my father so I should not sample the vegan brownie.

I did not actually say that but I thought it.

He was going to die soon anyway.

22

I need to go to Darwin, Oren said, walking into the bathroom. I was in the shower, playing with a stray hair on the glass door as I waited for my conditioner to set. He surprised me. I thought he was cleaning up after dinner.

Don't do anything stupid, I said as I looked up at him through the foggy glass.

Is that a Darwin Awards joke? he said, smiling, opening the mirror cabinet and getting out his toothbrush.

I joined the ends of the long brown hair together. The resulting shape looked a little like California.

You should come, he said, running his toothbrush under the faucet. I'll be in meetings but you could explore. Brenda told me about this travel company. Why don't you call them?

I pressed my finger where San Francisco would be and dragged the hair across the door, leaving a streak.

The next week we flew to the Northern Territory, which looks like a square with the top side shredded. After spending the night in Darwin in a hotel that smelled like sweat, Oren walked to his meeting and I sat on a black leather bench in the lobby with a small suitcase and a water bottle. A man named Gav was supposed to pick me up and drive me several hours east to Arnhem Land, where I would stay for two nights and see twenty-eight-thousand-year-old cave art. The stench in the hotel was overwhelming.

I wrote Abby to tell her I wouldn't be reachable as I was headed into the wilderness. I considered the word *wilderness* and how it sounded dark, quiet, and feminine, whereas the word *bush* was loud and prickly.

The man at reception hung up the phone and was now drawing on a map that he was showing to two older women in almost identical beige outfits that looked brand new. The shorter one kept shaking her head, disapproving of the day's plan, and the one holding a plastic bag seemed irritated with her traveling companion and looked to the desk clerk for validation. I wondered if the man went home to anyone who had to listen to him vent about the guests or if he lived alone because he couldn't bear talking to anyone at the end of the day.

Edie?

I spun around to see a large brass belt buckle engraved with the face of a crocodile and quickly stood up. The man reached out his hand and said, I'm Gav. Pleasure to meet you.

His hand was large and leathery, like a baseball mitt, and completely enveloped mine. His face looked like a ripe pomegranate, dusty pink and spotted, and his thin hair stuck out on all sides. He also wore beige, but unlike the women at the desk, his clothing was wrinkled and stained. Hands on his hips, he smiled and asked if I was ready to go. He had a tiny ball of spit on one corner of his mouth and he flicked his tongue to the side to capture it.

In his mammoth grip, my suitcase looked like a purse, and he tossed it into the trunk of his car with ease. I hope you weren't expecting a safari Jeep, he said, starting the motor. Boots Safari, name confuses people sometimes. Boots Camry, more like it. He chuckled.

Is Boots your last name? It was, and he adjusted the air-conditioning vents.

As he drove out of Darwin onto a two-lane highway, I stared out the window. Unlike the reddish-brown hues of Western Australia, the Northern Territory was green and tropical. Palm trees lined the road like soldiers. Pairs of large brown birds gathered in the road to pick at the pavement and, at the last minute, flew out of the way of approaching cars. They were noisy, with high-pitched calls and enormous wingspans. Whistling kites, Gav said. He told me they ate insects off the road, lizards if they were lucky.

We stopped for morning tea at a roadhouse with tiki font signage. Three Aboriginal men in black shirts were drinking coffee at a rusty round table on the porch, and they watched us from the moment the car stopped until we walked up the front steps. G'day Gav, the one with the bandanna said as we walked past.

How ya going? Gav responded, holding open the screen door for me. I got a sparkling water and Gav a flat white, and we sat on the opposite end of the porch, Gav's back to the threesome.

Blackfellas know me around here, he said. I'm one of them.

I looked puzzled, because Gav was white.

Was raised out here in the bush, he explained. Me and my mum and dad and my sister. I'll show you. He scrolled through his phone and showed me a photograph of an old newspaper article. The headline was "Frontier Women of Arnhem Land," and the accompanying photo was of a white woman propping one foot up on a log. She was holding a shotgun and wore a button-down shirt with the sleeves rolled up. She looked like she was laughing.

Your mom?

He nodded. My dad started Boots Safari. White people aren't allowed in here without permission. And I'm their ticket in.

I didn't understand.

It's native land up here, Edie, he said, owned and operated by Aboriginals. The way the whole country should be, I reckon. They let me carry on with Dad's company. I owe them my life.

Soon we were back in the Camry, speeding down the highway. I pulled the seat belt tighter and tried to imagine Gav in San Francisco.

After an hour or so, we reached a town called Jabiru, and he turned off the main road to cross the East Alligator River into a territory that could only be accessed with permission from the traditional landowners.

Not many white people have been allowed out here, Gav said. He shook his head and added, Understandable if you think about it. If I were a Blackfella, I would be done with white people altogether. Our two countries are similar that way, you reckon? White people coming in and tearing everything apart.

I held my arms across my chest as the car sped down the rugged dirt road, at the end of which we were met by a young white married couple who managed the lodge. I was given a small bedroom on the upper level of the modest structure, while Gav set up his tent behind the lodge, next to the sundial.

The next day, after a breakfast of Weet-Bix, poached eggs, and floppy bacon, Gav gave me a notebook called "Species Checklist" and a blue pen with a chewed top. You can write down what you see, he said as we approached the Jeep he had borrowed for the day. He opened the door for me and added, It helps you to remember, tapping his temple.

He said this as if it were a new concept. Writing things down in order to remember.

We drove down rocky wet paths, through mud, and over anthills, then got out to climb up and over boulders to find ancient cave drawings.

Those things will kill you, Gav said, pointing to small black spots on wet rocks. He slammed his foot down hard as if killing a cockroach and the spots jumped. I let out a high-pitched yelp. Cane toads, he said. One touch and you're dead. He slapped his hands together and laughed. I frantically scanned the ground near my feet.

We climbed to the side of a mountain overlooking the East Alligator River. My temples were throbbing and my elbow creases were dripping with sweat. I asked Gav if we could sit down somewhere in the shade, to take a break from the sun.

Of course, he said, but first you've got to try this. He handed me a folded green leaf covered in hundreds of green ants. It's like medicine.

I shook my head and took a sip of water. He said, Suit yourself, and popped the whole thing in his mouth. Minty, he said with his mouth full and a few stray ants crawling over his chin.

We sat at the entrance to a cave, under eight or nine red handprints and a very realistic drawing of a sailboat. That's contact art, Gav explained. That was done after the white man came.

I tried to imagine what it would be like to live out here, among the thorny trees and caves and lizards, and suddenly have people show up who looked nothing like you, wearing clothing, having boats and guns, wanting your land.

It must have been scary, I said.

Gav spit on the ground. Scary for who?

The Aboriginal people, I said.

Yup, he said. Fucking shit.

He asked me if I owned a gun. I shook my head. Thought everyone owned a gun in America, he said. He tossed a pebble and asked me if I wanted to hear a story about a knife.

Years ago, Gav made himself a long knife and carried it in a specially made pack that he wore under his shirt. So he could reach behind his neck, down his shirt, and whip it out as needed, he explained.

I pulled it once on a bloke in Caracas, he said. I was there with Marie, my then wife. We were in a real dangerous area and got a ride from this guy. It was a real bad area, real bad. He started driving us the wrong way, into a place that looked even worse than the first place.

Gav brushed a fly off his cheek and said, Edie, you understand this. I have a very good sense of where I am, a good directional sense, you know what I'm saying?

I nodded. He was right. He did seem to have an extraordinary sense of direction, which was no surprise given he grew up in the wilderness.

Gav continued: I made him pull over. I knew he was going the wrong way. That's when I pulled out my knife and jammed it into the side of his rib cage.

I braced my hands on my knees. I was not expecting that. You stabbed him?

You bet I did, Edie. I jam the knife right into his side and I tell him, You're the first to die if we get mugged. I know you're not taking us to the right place. Turn around and drive us where I asked you to drive us.

I noticed that Gav sometimes switched to present tense in the middle of a story. Dad did that. It drove Mom crazy. She was a stickler for grammar, even at the expense of a good story.

Jesus, what happened? I asked Gav.

The bloke turns the car around, he's got blood pouring out of him, and takes us where we need to go. We get out of the van and I see the guy get his phone out. He was calling his gang. I tell Marie to run. We stayed low that night and got out of town the next day. Didn't want to stay around there too long with stabbing the guy and whatnot.

I removed my sun hat and wiped my brow. Is that it? I asked. Or did he find you?

Nah, he didn't find us.

We both looked at the ground.

I never travel without that knife, I tell you, Edie.

I asked him if he had it now.

Nah. No one's gonna kill me out here. He laughed. Unless you turn out to be the violent type.

Some of the cave drawings seemed to tell gruesome stories, but mostly they were animals and people and always surrounded by ocher handprints that made it look like hundreds of children were trapped inside, trying to push their way out. Gav took a photo of me in front of a long row of stick figures. As he handed back my phone, he said, You know, Edie, I've done some things I'm not proud of.

Sorry? I slid my phone in my pocket and squinted at him. The sunlight was blocking part of his face.

He scratched the back of his neck and said, You're about the age of my daughter. You girls don't get it yet, but when you get older you'll look back at your life and— He stopped talking and pointed at the green pandanus behind me. I turned to see a small rock wallaby bound past. A squirrel in a kangaroo costume.

Everyone makes mistakes, I said quietly, turning back to face him.

He looked up at the sky for a moment and then back at me. I guess it's just learning which ones you can live with, he said.

We said nothing for a while. I thought that life was about moving from one thing to another, all the previous things falling down behind you, but I was beginning to see that this was not the case at all. That in fact every action, every thought, and every word uttered, they all stayed with you and formed a sort of jumbled collage. This thought frightened me.

We crossed a stream, stepping from rock to rock. He led me up a hill to see hundreds of small piles of gray rocks that seemed to have been arranged with care. Nothing was growing up here. It looked like the surface of the moon. Gav pointed at the rock piles and said that kids might have done this thousands of years ago. Maybe they were set up as part of a ceremony. He said he brought an archaeologist from Oxford up here last year who couldn't explain it. Gav looked smug, thinking about this.

I squatted down next to one of the piles and stared at it. Gav said, The Oxford bloke said he's fairly certain they were set up by humans. But I like to think it could be some kind of leftover thing from some sort of natural catastrophe. Or aliens of course. He laughed. Hell, we don't know anything. He smiled and rubbed his eyes.

It's so quiet up here, I said.

Feels like the end of the world, ay?

Dad once told me, while tweezing a splinter out of my big toe, that you could never describe something while it was in the process of occurring. That only afterward you would find the words. I wondered if Fiona said things like this to her children. I didn't know why I was thinking of her, out here in the quiet.

Many weeks later, after this trip to the Northern Territory, I read in the news that archaeologists had discovered the oldest known grinding stone in Arnhem Land, two and a half meters down, proving that humans arrived in Australia much earlier than previously thought. There was no mention of the rock piles, nor the cave art. What they were looking for was buried much deeper down.

23

Back in Perth, I had work to do. I needed to research the positive impact of nature exposure on impoverished children who live in cities. I also needed to learn about watersheds. I took a bus to the main library downtown and told the woman at the desk about my assignment. How sad, she said, as she stood up and removed her glasses. Can you imagine never going to a park?

She was tall and thin, had ice-cream cone earrings, and wore her short hair in a pigtail on the top of her head like a hook. As she escorted me to the nonfiction section, she told me she was from Queensland and still liked to climb trees when she had the chance. Her parents still lived there. Her younger brother was recently ticketed for drunk driving and he'd probably never even read a single book. Not one.

Thankfully a man with chapped lips and droopy eyelids approached her to ask about gardening books.

It turned out people with limited exposure to fresh air and trees are more likely to suffer from depression and obesity. And it was easy to build a case for repairing the environment. I thought about using *watershed* in a clever double-meaning kind of way but decided against it. Instead I named the campaign "Nature and Nurture" and suggested a logo of two trees hugging each other. I wrote a strategy for an online fund-raising and social media campaign, corporate sponsorship ideas, sample solicitation letters, and t-shirt slogans.

It was getting late. I was hungry, my wrists hurt, and the sun was beginning to go down. I left the library.

G'day, said the bus driver as I boarded.

Hello, I responded as I brushed off some crumbs on the front seat near a sign that said SEE SOMETHING. SAY SOMETHING. ANTISOCIAL BEHAVIOR WILL NOT BE TOLERATED. The bus had just a few other passengers, including Fiona, who caught me by surprise. A few rows away, she was staring out the window with her baby on her lap. The baby pointed at me and made a sound. When Fiona turned and spotted me, I smiled and she turned away, as if in disgust. The bus lurched forward and I held my stomach. Fiona hated me.

At the next stop, a woman with bright pink cheeks boarded. She looked out of breath. Her hair was long and white, with pink and purple streaks. She held her SmartRider card up to the scanner and sighed with relief when it beeped. Clutching a bar near the rear doors, she held her purse close to her body without taking a seat.

Trying to forget about Fiona, I opened my news app. Something horrible had happened in the United States. An illustrated map showed the locations of the bodies. Maybe I should use a graph for the environmental organization. I got a text from Abby. It was a link to a video of cats being startled by cucumbers. The president was planning to meet with the families.

Someone pushed the button signaling the driver to pull over at the next stop. The back door opened and a piercing scream broke the silence like a meteorite crash in the desert.

It's ripped off! Oh my god!

I looked behind me and realized the scream was coming from the woman with the white hair with the pink and purple streaks. The news rippled among the passengers that the bus door had torn off the entire nail of the woman's big toe.

A passenger ran over to her. He had thickly accented English and said, Come with me, I'm going to help you. He held up the woman as she stumbled out of the bus and over to the bus shelter. Her foot was covered in blood. She was sobbing. Through my window, I watched the man as he helped the woman onto a bench and propped up her bloody foot on his knee. The blood was flowing onto his pants. The woman was shaking and howling. I glanced back at Fiona, who looked frightened and held her baby close. She wouldn't look at me.

The bus driver had gone outside and was now crouched next to the woman. He reached into his pocket and offered his handkerchief to the man, who quickly wrapped it around her foot. The driver boarded the bus for a moment to call someone. One of my passengers is hurt, he said loudly into the phone. We will be here for a while. Yes. Thank you.

I removed my wallet from my bag and searched the pockets for Band-Aids, but came up with nothing. I left my bag on my seat and went outside. I asked the man, still holding the woman's foot, if he needed an ambulance. He said no, the woman just called her husband. He was on his way.

The woman with the white hair with the pink and purple streaks looked at me and scooted over on the bench, as if to make room. I sat down next to her and couldn't think of what to say. I'm sorry I don't have any Band-Aids, I said.

She collapsed on my shoulder and started to cry again. I can't believe this happened, she moaned. I'm supposed to go hiking next weekend.

I sat very still.

One by one, the remaining passengers disembarked. An older lady had tissues and stories of awful toenail injuries from when she was a ballerina. Toes heal quickly, trust me, she said.

A passenger with a long blond ponytail was on her way from wait-ressing downtown to coaching gymnastics. I'll be late but it doesn't matter, she said.

A young man dressed in all black came over to the bench and handed the woman an unopened bottle of water. You should be a doctor, he said to the man with blood on his pants.

The man's cheeks turned red. I hope to be one soon, he said.

It turned out he was in medical school up the road. Everyone laughed, including the injured woman, who shook her head in disbelief and looked at me. What are the chances? she said.

Fiona handed a bandage to the woman. Of course Fiona had a bandage. She was prepared for any emergency, rarely startled by anything. I started to say something to her, but she turned and walked away briskly with her baby, down the hill.

The husband arrived. Oh, Junie Bug, he said, putting his hand to her cheek.

His wife started crying again. All these people took such good care of me, she said.

Of course they did, Junie Bug, of course they did.

Everyone said goodbye to the woman with the white hair with the pink and purple streaks and got back on the bus, returning to their original seats. I looked out the window the rest of the way home. Fiona was on the corner, waiting to cross the street. Baby on her shoulders now, they were both laughing.

The article said that many of those people who were killed were having the best night of their lives.

24

One Wednesday I forgot all about Dad. Then I went to bed with a book. In the middle of a paragraph was the phrase *severed head of a ceramic doll*. I remembered everything with a terrible shock, like slipping on ice. I pinched the skin on the palm of my hand until it burned and listened to something run across the roof. Over and over.

25

After Oren left for work, I read an article online. "Fatal Bear Attack in Wyoming." A man's body had been found outside of a cave in Bridger-Teton. Most of the flesh had been ripped from his bones. The man's name was Seth Lister.

My first Thanksgiving away at college, I spent the long weekend with a girl named Lauren Lister at her family's house on Long Island. We weren't particularly close, but she and I worked together at the campus dry cleaners. When she learned I was planning to stay at school over the holiday weekend, she said, That's sad. You should come home with me. Her childhood room was very girly, with lace curtains and yellow rose wallpaper, which she used to peel back to write the names of boys she liked, as well as anything else she needed to get off her chest. *Dave. Carlos. Mom is annoying. I wish Claire would break her arm.* I slept on the bottom bunk and stared up at the glow-in-the-dark adhesive butterflies.

Lauren had a brother named Seth who was still in high school and lurked in doorways. He was the kind of person who would have hidden behind a tree at someone's funeral. I got stuck sitting across from him on Thanksgiving and had to watch him gnaw on a turkey leg until it was bare, at which point he deposited the large bone beside his plate on the faded purple tablecloth and wiped his mouth on the sleeve of his plaid flannel shirt.

He leaned over and whispered to me across the table: I can't wait to get away from all this.

I don't think I had heard him say one word since we arrived the night before. I don't know what you mean, I responded, scooping more cranberry sauce onto my plate.

This is bullshit, all this luxury, he said, rolling his eyes. I looked over at their father, who was at the end of the table emptying a packet of Splenda into his coffee. The older neighbor couple on either side of him kept interrupting each other as they talked about a local politician they had run into at a bowling alley. Lauren was in the kitchen helping her mom defrost a store-bought pound cake.

Seth continued. As soon as I graduate, I'm selling all my stuff and buying a car. I wanna drive cross-country and have time to think, you know? Gotta stop eating meat too. This stuff is disgusting, he said, gesturing at the devoured leg.

You looked like you enjoyed it, I responded, wiping my mouth with a paper towel, which I then crumpled and held in my fist under the table.

I did. He shook his head. That's what's wrong with everything, Edie. Humans just take whatever they want. We don't even have to kill for it, we just go to Costco and buy dead animals wrapped in plastic for a holiday commemorating the slaughter of millions of Native Americans.

I don't think it was millions, I said. Seth glared at me.

Lauren came back to clear the table. Hey, Edie, wanna give me a hand?

As we stood at the kitchen sink scraping remaining food into the trash, she apologized for her brother. He's such a creep sometimes. You should see what he writes in his diary.

You read his diary? I asked, stacking dishes in the dishwasher. Only once, she said, when I thought he might blow up the school.

Seth ended up doing exactly what he said he'd do. Two weeks after he graduated from high school, he took off in a used Accord with a large duffel bag and a gas stove and drove west.

The article said that park rangers shot and killed the bear they thought was responsible for the attack. They weren't certain this was the bear that had ripped Seth apart. But they killed it anyway. They had to do something.

*

After reading this, I walked to the post office to mail a letter to Abby. Fiona was gardening and I told her a guy I once knew was eaten by a bear. I said it was a strange coincidence, that I knew him. Livvie popped up from behind a bush and said, Eaten?

Well, more like ripped apart to death, I said, scratching the air for effect. Livvie ran to her mother and buried her head in her shoulder. You reckon that was a good choice? Fiona asked me sternly, as she stroked her daughter's hair. I mean really, Edie. You shouldn't say such a thing to a child.

I looked at the scene, of a mother consoling a daughter. Fiona wore a sun hat large enough to shade both their heads. I told her I was sorry and that I was going to the post office. No, they didn't need anything.

26

I set my alarm. I had a call with someone in San Francisco about a fund-raising letter. It was urgent. No one was responding to their campaign. They had sent me the copy and it was terrible. Four long paragraphs using phrases like *strategic planning* and *developmentally disabled citizens*. No wonder no money was coming in.

They had three people on the call, huddled around a speakerphone in a conference room. They said they could hear the birds over the phone. I told them what I thought of the letter, which was that no one who might give ten dollars cares about high-level strategy. People want to hear one story about one person who was given a chance. And no one reads paragraphs. Put the second sentence in bold font and add a p.s. These are the only two things anyone will read. Especially in an email. This has been proven in national studies in philanthropy.

One of the men chuckled and said he had been trying to tell the others this very thing. Without even seeing this man's face, I could tell he was the kind of person who claimed other people's ideas as his own. It reminded me of a sociology class in college. The professor split us into groups and assigned each group a research project, which we then had to present in front of the class. I worked hard on the assignment, which had something to do with perception of taxation levels. During our presentation, Brad from Connecticut took credit for my ideas. Not once, but over and over again. He seemed to have convinced himself that my work was his and now wanted to prove this to everyone else. That was my idea actually, I said, in front of the class. People snickered and I realized no one cared where the idea came from. They just wanted to see the jerk pace back and forth in his form-fitting polo. Even the professor was smitten.

For the next class assignment, I plagiarized the whole thing. I copied entire paragraphs out of books and pieced the whole thing together like an AIDS quilt. The professor asked to see me, and after she rightly accused me of cheating, I told her I didn't see the difference between what the jerk did and what I did. She asked if I had sacrificed this writing assignment to prove a point and I said not intentionally, but now that she'd pointed it out, yes, that is what I must have done. I redid the assignment and the professor asked me to be her teaching assistant the following term.

I'd be happy to take a stab at the letter, I said to the men on the phone. They said they wanted the tone to be friendly and I said I'm good at that. The chuckler requested I send him the draft as soon as I could.

After I hung up the phone, I closed my eyes and lay back on the couch. It was still very early in the morning.

The wind rumbled outside, starting soft then getting louder, like a motorcycle driving past. Oren was probably still sleeping, even with the sound of the birds and the wind. It was winter, and I had purchased a knit blanket at a craft fair that I now pulled up over my robe to my chin. It was made by a resident at a domestic violence shelter and it smelled like an attic.

After Dad died I had to send an email with the funeral details to a list of extended family and friends that Mom had provided. I debated the subject heading because I knew the email would sit in inboxes before and after other subjects of varied urgency. Mom had suggested *Sad News*, but I thought this should be reserved for a note regarding a canceled vacation or sold-out movie tickets. I settled on *Paul Richter's Funeral*. I told Oren it would make a good band name and he said thank god I had a sense of humor.

Hey, scoot over. Oren gave me a start. I hadn't realized he was kneeling beside me. Good call? he asked, yawning. He curled up beside me, pulling the blanket over to cover half his body. He laid his head on my chest. It's too early, he said. I don't want to go to work.

I tried to imagine him not being there. Not existing at all.

He said, I had a dream our love was a shape. Like some amorphous, constantly changing thing, floating around behind us. It was cool. He stretched his leg out and then dropped it over my legs. Like, can you imagine? If our love was a physical thing that we could look at?

The wind revved up and sped by.

I love hearing your heartbeat, he said, squeezing me slightly.

It's better than not hearing my heartbeat, I said.

Oren sat up abruptly and glared at me. Can't we just have a moment without you making a weird joke?

I'm sorry, I said. I'm tired.

He grabbed my hand and said, Sometimes I really need you, Edie. And it's ok for you to need me too. It's not that complicated.

I didn't know what to say. He left the room and turned on the shower.

There are two kinds of stories. There's the kind where someone changes, and there's the kind where someone stays exactly the same.

27

Leaving the house, I noticed the corner of a padded envelope poking out from under the welcome mat. Mail from Abby. I tucked it under my arm and walked to the park.

That evening, several families with young children were huddled around a picnic table. Wrapped gifts sat in a pile next to the table on the concrete. The smell of cooked sausages mixed with the smell of eucalyptus. Two children chased each other, one of them holding a cupcake. A woman on a blanket watched them go around and around as she tied a scarf around her neck.

I watched four young coots swimming in the lake alongside their mother. An older woman in a motorized wheelchair pulled up next to me and said, When coot chicks beg their mother for food, the mother sometimes pecks or starves them to death. Then she asked if I had children.

A flock of long-billed corellas filled a nearby tree and squawked loudly. One flew down from a long branch and searched the grass for fallen berries. It was white with a ragged red line across its neck that made it look like its throat had been slashed. I sat on a bench holding the package, considering its contents. It might have to do with Abby's latest obsession, like a new spice or another book about spirituality. Finally I ripped it open. Inside was a note and something in bubble wrap.

> *Dear Edie,*
> *You've always done what you want to do, and I mean that as a compliment. Dad admired that about you. He used to tell me to watch and learn from you, because you never let anyone take advantage of you. I just wanted to write and say thank you for being an awesome big sister. I miss you.*
> *Abs*

My eye twitched. Inside the bubble wrap was a framed photo of Dad and me, sitting next to each other on the grass. He was in a white t-shirt and jeans, his back resting against a tree, holding his folded glasses in one hand, his other arm around me. He was squinting and his face was unshaven. I was sitting with my knees up and ankles crossed. My hair was shorter then, and my long bangs covered one eye. I wore jeans and a brown jacket that I didn't recognize at first, but then I remembered it was Wendy's.

When I stayed with Wendy after the breakup, she called my parents to tell them she was worried about me. Dad flew out the next day. During his illness, Dad spoke about this trip a few times. He had forgotten the reason for his visit and had reimagined it as an adventure that the two of us had together. I loved going to Boston with you, Edie, he'd say. What a beautiful city, what a great idea. I would agree and tell him my favorite parts, like the cannoli in the North End and the portraits at the Gardner Museum. We reminisced about something that had never happened.

Now, as I sat on the bench at the lake, I thought of my mind as a depository holding my own memories of my father and also memories my father passed on to me, both real and imaginary. In my death, this part of him would die again. I inhaled the cold air and turned my head to look back at the birthday party. The children were too young to remember this day. I collected their faces and the way their arms swung from side to side as they ran in circles.

28

Jamie the driving instructor died.

Oren brought this piece of news home from work casually, as one might a slice of leftover conference room birthday cake.

He's dead? How?

At the dinner table apparently. Heart attack or something, they're not sure. I saw Brenda coming out of a meeting. She remembered you took a lesson with him.

Oren left the kitchen and I continued to stir the risotto. I switched on the ceiling fan to block out the scratching sound in the wall.

A funeral was planned for the following Saturday.

The first time I had driven past Karrakatta Cemetery was with Jamie. On Railway Road, across from the train station, it was hard to miss. Thousands of gray tombstones, haphazardly scattered like Legos, were visible behind the long row of eucalyptus trees. He told me this was where priests used to do midnight burials for victims of small-pox. Heath Ledger was buried at Karrakatta, along with some racist politicians, Jamie said. He said you could tell a lot about a city by visiting its libraries and cemeteries.

A small group of people was huddled near the entrance to the cemetery café, called But First, Coffee. A woman in a navy suit with a clipboard approached me and asked if I were here to attend a funeral and, if so, which one.

Jamie, I said tentatively, realizing I never learned his last name.

Family and friends are gathering in the chapel, she said. Down this path, take a left at Dench Chapel and the Book of Remembrance, you won't miss it.

Country music was playing softly in the background. Something about coming home to the land I love. A young man with greased-back hair and a crooked tie handed me a program, and I took a seat in the back row.

Two women in front of me were arguing about step dancing. That's Scottish, not Irish, the one in the blue hat said disparagingly.

No, it was Irish, the younger one said, tucking her red hair behind her ear.

Was there heaps of bagpipe?

Yes.

Were they using their arms?

Yes.

That's Scottish dancing, I promise you.

The younger one sighed.

The service began with a prayer. I bowed my head and spotted a spider on the pew in front of me. The minister described Jamie as a legendary hero whose life achievements knew no boundaries. His smile, humor, and limitless knowledge would be sadly missed by all. A gifted musician, a lively storyteller, a dog lover. Let us rise. Please be seated.

Oren stayed home. He couldn't see the point, which now, at a funeral for a man with whom I briefly shared a car, was a point I could see.

His daughter spoke. Bronnie. Twenty-eight on the twenty-eighth. She wore a shapeless black dress and had stringy brown hair and bloodshot eyes. Voice trembling, she read from her notes. Her father once hid raw eggs in their backyard on Easter. Children stepped on them, Mother got upset, Father stood in the corner laughing. He was close with his dog, Timba, who liked to sit in the passenger seat of his beat-up Holden. He taught high school science until he missed driving so much he switched paths. His eyes twinkled when he was happy, and nothing made him angrier than people who were cruel to animals. He lived for his two grandsons, she said, pausing to blow her nose. He touched many people's lives. Just look at this room, she said, looking down at her notes.

She said it wasn't fair that he died so quickly. There was so much she would have said to him, and she would now say all of those things. She turned to face the casket.

I loved you, Dad, she said quietly. I didn't tell you this often enough. I don't know why and I'm sorry.

I crossed my legs then uncrossed them and rested my elbows on my knees. I felt uncomfortable that she was addressing a dead man directly.

When Timba died, I told you to get another dog and you yelled at me. I don't blame you. It was a stupid thing to say and I'm sorry. I know how much you loved that dog. I'm sorry I never apologized for that. She inhaled her snot.

A toddler in the front yelled, I don't want to! Bronnie looked up, momentarily confused.

You were right about a lot of things, Bronnie continued. Even when I didn't want to hear it.

She began to sob. I wish I could have told you all this, she said.

An older woman in a purple dress approached Bronnie, whispered in her ear, then escorted her back to her seat.

A friend of Jamie's talked about Jamie's fondness for bad jokes and then proceeded to tell a joke about a snail. The minister thanked him and said something about the healing power of good memories.

I decided to skip the reception and went to the cemetery café. They were playing Frank Sinatra. I sat at a table near a bookshelf. It was a very depressing collection of books, which was surprising on the one hand, but then again, maybe that's what people wanted to read while sipping coffee at a cemetery. *Dying Young, The Bridges of Madison County*, something called *Color Is the Suffering of Light*. Between *One Flew Over the Cuckoo's Nest* and a glossy paperback with a gold dagger on the binding was a book about cocker spaniels. I pulled it out. The cover had a photograph of a brown cocker spaniel, its eyes large, brown, and sparkling. I pulled the book close to me and smelled it.

Are you Canadian?

A blue-eyed, gray-haired woman in an apron was holding my soy latte. I noticed your accent, she said, as she set it down on the small round table. She wore a silver ring with a large green stone.

I shook my head as I returned the book to the shelf.

The woman waited for a moment and then walked away.

The song "Luck Be a Lady" came on. I stirred my latte with the tiny silver spoon and looked out the window. Two magpies were pecking at the grass at the foot of a large eucalyptus tree.

29

I was preparing an organic chicken for dinner that I had purchased from a farm up north. Two hours in the car. I had washed it and massaged it with coconut oil and was shoving half a lemon and some rosemary into the cavity, when Oren walked in with a large pet crate.

Look who's here, he announced.

Hold on, I said, and tucked small potatoes under the wings, tied the legs together with brown string, sprinkled turmeric over the whole thing, and put it in the oven. I washed my hands and looked over at him as I dried my hands on a filthy red-and-white-striped tea towel.

Look who's here, he repeated.

Is that a cat?

Edie, it's Frisbee.

I had forgotten about the cat, whose existence had not been mentioned since it went to live with Mom and Abby in San Francisco and we flew to Perth. I did not miss this cat, due to the fact that I had never enjoyed it to begin with. This was the breakup kitten that Oren had adopted in Boston. It came with us to San Francisco, on the airplane in a soft carrier Oren had bought from a company whose motto was *Life Without Cats is No Life at All*. The carrier turned out to be impossible to clean and also poorly designed, as the cat could unzip it from the inside. The cross-country flight was stressful, as one of us had to pinch the carrier closed at all times so the cat wouldn't roam the aisles. Now it had followed us here, to our kitchen in Perth.

Poor little guy, Oren said. He needs a bath. I did it to surprise you, he added, leaving the cat in the crate and coming over to hug me.

I am surprised, I said. How did he get here? He's so old.

He pinched me and said, Well, he didn't have to fly the plane.

Seriously, though, Edie, you would not believe the amount of paper-work required to bring a cat into Australia. You'd think he was eight pounds of cocaine, he continued. He then described all the effort and secrecy involved in surprising one's wife with a cat that she never liked. Flea treatments, rabies vaccine, checking for worms, you wouldn't be-lieve it, Edie.

I knelt down beside the crate. He looks filthy, I said.

He's been in quarantine in Sydney for ten days, Oren said. You gotta give the little guy a break. Hey, let's let him out in the bathroom and then we can give him a bath.

Do you mind if I skip the bath? I've got the chicken going—I gestured toward the oven—and I was going to make a salad with an oil-free dressing.

Are you serious? Oren looked upset. He took the crate to the bathroom and turned on the tub.

As I tore lettuce into small pieces and tossed them in the salad spinner, I remembered another time Oren surprised me. It was my birthday and he invited my coworkers to secretly meet us at a Tex-Mex bar after work. That afternoon, I had gotten into an argument with one of them. The argument had to do with a new intern. The coworker had hired this intern after meeting her at a singles event and, realizing he didn't have any projects for her, assigned her to me. This was indicative of a larger issue at this particular organization, which was that not enough thought was put into hiring anyone, so people floated around the office with a mix of insecurity and boastfulness, a need to show off, a direct result of not feeling needed. This coworker didn't understand why I didn't want an intern. Everyone needs interns, he said.

Then why don't you keep her? I said.

She's a better fit for you, he said, as if we were trying on jeans.

I told him I had to get final copy of the annual report to the design firm, I didn't have time for an intern, and I was going to go home to finish writing. Another problem with this office was that people worked wherever they wanted, and no one was ever where they claimed to be.

The coworker, remembering the surprise at the Tex-Mex bar, said, No, please don't go home, I'll take the intern. And the argument ended just like that. One month later, the intern and my coworker were seen holding hands and the coworker was asked to resign.

When Oren and I arrived at the Tex-Mex birthday party, I saw my coworkers gathered at the bar and assumed they had planned a night out without me. When the human resources director presented me with a digital music gift voucher and wished me a happy birthday, I looked at Oren with surprise. I didn't understand why he thought I would want to celebrate my birthday with my coworkers.

I whisked together tahini, lemon juice, and Dijon mustard and heard Oren talking to the cat.

We ate silently on the couch, while the cat roamed the house and rubbed against chair legs. Something in our relationship was making me angry. I found a tiny sharp chicken bone wandering around my mouth and used my tongue to lodge it under my upper lip. I was suddenly disgusted by this moment on the couch, with the chicken bone, with Oren, and of course with the stupid cat. I washed the dishes aggressively and stomped off to the bedroom.

What the hell is wrong with you? Oren grabbed my arm and flung me around. I shook it off and sat down on the bed.

What are you talking about? I said.

Something's different about you, since we came here. I knew we shouldn't have come here. It was too soon, he said quietly. He sat down on the other side of the bed, our backs facing each other.

It's good we moved, I said. It's not that. It's not anything, really.

He lay down and touched my thigh. Edie, I feel like you don't talk to me when something is bothering you.

Nothing's bothering me, I said, scooting away from his hand.

He stood up and came around to kneel on the floor in front of me. You see, I know that's not true. I know you well enough to know when something's wrong. You're off. More off than normal. He smiled, sat cross-legged on the floor, and said, All I want is for you to trust me and talk to me.

The cat walked in the room and rubbed itself against Oren's thigh. He scratched its ear.

And you thought the cat would help? I asked him.

I just thought it would be fun, having Frisbee in Perth. It seemed like we might need a little pick-me-up.

Sometimes Oren sounded like an old lady.

The cat left the room.

Do you miss your dad?

I didn't say anything.

I miss your dad, he said, running his hand through his hair. He would love it here, don't you think? He'd love the coffee. And the way every-one has time to talk.

I reached for the small red tube of ointment on my bedside table, squeezed a tiny amount onto my fingertip and rubbed it on my lips.

Edie? He touched my leg. Why don't you ever talk about your dad?

I stood up and turned to him. I'm sorry, what are we talking about? The cat or my dad?

Come on, don't be that way.

No really. I'm asking because I don't know what's happening. Am I happy about the cat? No. Am I happy about my father dying? No.

The problem with you, Edie, is that you don't let anyone in.

This was not the first time he had said this.

What you don't seem to understand is that I love you, and I want to help you. I'm sorry about the cat, ok? I thought it would help. Not help exactly, but I don't know, make you smile or something.

You thought a cat I never liked would make me smile?

You don't have to be such a bitch about it. He rolled his eyes. Do you know what a pain in the ass it was getting a cat into Australia?

I know, I said. You told me all about it.

I walked to the dresser and put my earrings in a small, wobbly blue ceramic bowl that Abby made me for my twentieth birthday. The cat was lying on top of the dresser and this startled me. I didn't realize it had returned.

I'm getting upset, Oren said, stating the obvious. You're hurting my feelings. It's not my fault your dad got sick.

I turned to face him and he held up both of his hands in surrender.

I'm sorry, he said, I didn't mean that.

You're right, I said. It's not your fault my dad got sick, and it's not your fault he died.

My body suddenly felt frozen to the ground. It felt like my feet had sunk straight into the earth. Oren walked up to me and put his arms around me. My arms stayed stuck to my sides.

Talk to me, Edie. You're not alone in all this. His head leaned against mine and his words vibrated against me.

Please don't touch me, I whispered.

He pulled back, held my shoulders, and looked at me. What? he said. What is it?

Don't touch me, I said. Give me some space.

He spoke in a low voice with his teeth clenched. Where do you expect me to go? How much more space do you fucking need? We're in Australia.

I wondered what that had to do with anything. He pulled off his t-shirt and jeans and got into bed, yanking the sheets up to his chin. I have a really fucking long day tomorrow, I'm going to go to bed.

You're already in bed, I said.

He flipped on his side and sighed loudly. You're not funny, Edie. Let me know if you ever want to talk like a human being.

I looked over at the cat, who was still on the dresser. It was staring at me.

I pulled on a sweatshirt and drove to the beach, closing my eyes as I passed the billboard for VINCENT GUERRA, #1 IN REAL ESTATE. I parked in an empty lot except for one construction truck and a Holden Cruze with fogged windows. No one else was there. Just some seagulls standing in groups of twos and threes at the shoreline. I ran down to the water, flipped off my sandals, and pulled my leggings up over my knees. The water was cooler than I expected and I dug my feet into the wet sand. Faint music was coming from the restaurant across the street. The waves were small and infrequent, and I let them push me back and forth as I thought about what Oren said. There wasn't a point in talking to him. What would be the point? It's not like I could change anything.

When I returned home, the cat was waiting in the hallway. It slinked over to smell my feet. That's the Indian Ocean, I whispered. I bet you've never smelled that before.

It was a new sensation.

30

Predictably, the person who brought the cat to Australia was not the person who spent the most time with it. In the mornings, after Oren left for work, I sat at the kitchen table eating my muesli with almond milk, clicking through articles or staring out the window. At first the cat startled me because I did not remember it was there and it looked out of place, like a chair floating in the ocean.

I began talking to it, which started the cycle of the cat rubbing itself against my leg, my asking a question it wouldn't answer, and the cat jumping up on my lap. Does that feel good, when I scratch your head? I didn't like talking to the cat when Oren was around, because it caused an I-told-you-so look I couldn't stand. Once he announced that the cat was becoming my emotional support animal, so I ignored the cat for three days.

It was a handsome animal, I could offer that much. A gray tabby, the color of morning fog, with light green eyes with yellow specks.

I wondered if the cat was trainable. The redheaded teenager at the pet supply store told me he taught his older cat to fetch. I bought three tiny fabric balls. I didn't mean for Oren to find out about this, but while sweeping one night, he found one under the kitchen sink and teased me, saying I secretly loved the cat.

I became preoccupied with what the cat was thinking. One night, it groomed itself next to me on the couch. I pulled it close and whispered, Do you even know where you are? It stared at me. I fell asleep with it on my chest and later awoke to a loud hissing and screeching sound. Frantic footsteps running across the roof, guttural growling and screaming. I'm sorry, I said to the cat. You're not alone.

The next day, I called the neighborhood council about the noise and the man said it was possums and that they sometimes kill each other during the "mating dance." That's what he called it. I asked if possums were dangerous to cats and he said generally it was the other way around. When I told him my cat's name was Frisbee and it came from America, he joked that it should be called Boomerang, now that it lived in Australia.

The cat occasionally meandered outside to chase cockroaches or stare at anthills. Sometimes it ran up the tree behind the house and watched the birds. That didn't last long, though. Soon, it stayed inside and mostly slept.

Frisbee seems depressed, I said to Oren one morning. It was curled up in the corner of our hall closet. Oren said he didn't think cats get depressed and that they are very food motivated. I told Oren he was having an episode of naive realism and he rolled his eyes.

It was clear the cat was losing weight, so I read online about sick cats. I could not determine whether the cat's eyes were sunken, if its paws were cool to the touch, or if its hind legs were weak. Finally the woman at the dry cleaners gave me the name of her vet and that is how we learned about the cancer.

31

Oren and I attended a Rosh Hashanah service. It was his idea. Let's see where all the Jews are hiding.

After the security guards checked our identification and my purse for explosives, the rabbi greeted us at the door. He was a bald Israeli with sweaty armpits, an untucked shirt, and thick glasses that were cracked on one side. We like to make you feel at home, he said, rolling his eyes, referring to the security. He and Oren spoke in Hebrew for a few minutes while I fiddled with my jacket zipper. We accepted prayer books from a French-braided teenager in a crushed blue velvet dress.

Oren always wanted to sit in the front of any room. Closer to the action, he said. We walked past many old people and families with children standing on the benches fiddling with their fathers' prayer shawls. Oren had worn his old Red Sox yarmulke for the occasion. It kept sliding off because he didn't have any pins and he used too much gel so his hair was like a waterslide.

The president of the board spoke about upcoming programs. There was a family picnic in Kings Park, a weekly meal delivery program for homebound seniors, and a Muslim-Jewish conversation series, which I first heard as *conversion series*. The treasurer seat was vacant and did we know anyone who liked money? We're all Jewish, he said, come on. Everyone laughed.

After the service, we walked to get Thai food. Oren said, I liked what he said in there about memory.

Who?

The rabbi, he said as he ducked under a jacaranda branch, his jacket brushing against it. Purple petals parachuted to the ground. He sounded exasperated. How Jews are commanded to remember, he said. How so many holidays have to do with recalling past events. The part about memories helping create the life we want.

He ran his fingertips along the top of a fence. It was cool, he said. Made me think about how memories don't have to haunt you, you can see them as building blocks or something. I don't know. I'm probably not saying it right. Anyway, it made me think about my mom.

He took my hand and we crossed the street.

He told me that he remembered with frightening clarity—he used those words, *frightening clarity*—the night his mother died and felt like he worked diligently to replace those memories with the ones where she was alive. But something the rabbi said made him feel he didn't have to reject these bad memories and instead see them as tools for the future.

And the same could be said about your dad, he said. You shouldn't worry if you think a lot about the night he died. It's ok. He squeezed my hand.

I yanked it away. I don't think you're saying it right, I said. I don't think that's what he was trying to say.

He stopped abruptly in front of a small gray apartment building and turned to me. Well, what do you think he was trying to say?

I brushed my hair back from my face and looked at Oren. Do you think you don't want to have kids because your mom died?

This was not a question I had considered asking before that moment.

He looked startled. What are you talking about?

An old man came out of the apartment building holding a trash bag and tossed it into one of the bins near the side entrance. Oren's voice got quieter. Edie? Why are you bringing this up right now? What does our decision to not have kids have to do with any of this?

It wasn't our decision, I said, looking at the ground. It was yours. And I'm just wondering if it's because your mom died.

The old man glanced over at us and returned inside.

Is this what's going on with you lately? Why you've been so weird?

I shrugged.

May I remind you our decision to not have children was a decision the two of us made together? Don't put that on me.

I looked at Oren and said, I just wonder if your mom were still alive, maybe you'd feel differently about having children.

He glared at me and said, Maybe if your dad were still alive, you wouldn't be such a bitch.

We stood stiffly next to each other in silence. Strangers waiting for a bus.

I didn't know why I had brought up the subject of having children. It wasn't something I had spent a lot of time thinking about. It was fair to say I had other things on my mind, things the size of tornados that blocked the view of something as small as hypothetical offspring.

I'm sorry, Oren said, scraping his shoe on the ground. I just don't know what's going on with you. I wish you'd let me in.

He removed a berry from the sole of his shoe, tossed it in the street, and then turned to me. He had tears in his eyes.

You're all I've got, Edie. What is going on with you?

He took my hands. I love you.

I nodded.

If you want to have a baby, I'm willing to talk about that.

I nodded again and stayed silent.

I knew I didn't want a baby. I also knew I should have put two bananas in my smoothie this morning. I would do that tomorrow.

I'm hungry, I said.

Oren put his arm around me and sighed. Let's go eat then.

32

We decided to do it on a Friday morning, when Oren could take time off work. He drove and I sat beside him, holding the cat on my lap. A hit song was on the radio. Oren quietly sang along, something about dentists and the dark. After he parked, he turned to me and said it never occurred to him that Frisbee would die here. He said he thought it would be a good thing, having the cat in Perth, that he was trying to help me, but maybe he didn't know how to help at all. His eyes were watery and he apologized several times.

It doesn't seem fair, I said to Oren. Our cat has cancer while possums are raping and killing each other on our roof.

He rested his hand on the cat, and I put my hand on top of his. I told him I felt empty. We sat like that for several minutes while the crows howled.

According to the vet, the cancer had come on quickly, almost with a vengeance, and no, we had told her, we didn't want to do more tests. Oren said that the cat was no spring chicken.

I had googled *Do cats prefer to die alone?*

Cats do not anticipate death.

They do not fear what they do not understand.

The decision to euthanize a cat is never an easy one.

Oren had emailed Abby and my mother to tell them the cat was sick and that we had made the decision to put it down. Abby called us and cried. Mom said the change in climate could have caused distress. I told her it was abdominal cancer, and she said the sun was very strong in Perth and they just got new wide-brimmed hats in the store. For children. Simply adorable. We had no idea.

The actual procedure was quick. The vet led us to a small room that looked like it was designed for the purpose of killing animals. There were books about astrology, healing, and interspecies friendships. A photograph of a sunset hung over a small purple couch. Oren and I sat down. The vet opened a cabinet and pulled down a small gray towel that she then handed to me. She pulled up a chair and told us that sometimes animals soil themselves when they pass. It's very natural, she said, but a towel can be useful. Oren wrapped the cat in the towel, so just its head was visible. Its eyes were foggy by now— they had been for well over a week. We didn't discuss who would hold the cat, but it ended up on my lap. The doctor explained that she would first administer a shot of pentobarbital in the leg, to render the cat unconscious. Then, once the cat was sleeping, she would give the second shot, the one that would stop the heart. We nodded. She asked if we had any questions. Oren asked how we'd know when it worked. She said the cat's heart would stop beating, and we would feel the cat's chest no longer rise and fall. You see how it moves up and down slightly now? We nodded. That will stop, she said. She asked if we were ready. She rested her hand on the cat and said, Losing a pet is never easy. The important thing is that we do what we can.

As I held the cat to wait for it to die, I closed my eyes. Oren put his arm around me.

My father gave a toast at our wedding. He welcomed Oren to the family, saying he already thought of him as a son but that this delicious cake and open bar made it official. Everyone laughed and Oren shook his hand and embraced him. I remember watching them hug, how long it seemed to go on, and how silent the room became. For a moment, this was their wedding, the joining of father and son. The two of them had whispered to each other, almost like they were exchanging something. Looking at them, I had felt a pang of envy or sadness.

I killed him.

It's over.

The vet touched my shoulder. It's over, she repeated.

I opened my eyes and looked at Oren, who was crying. I looked down at the cat in my arms and leaned down to press my face into its fur. It smelled like oatmeal. I felt dizzy.

After a few minutes, the vet asked if we were ready for her to take the body away and we agreed. Oren said the cat could be cremated with the other animals, no need for us to have any ashes. As she escorted us out of the room, she said, Frisbee was a perfect name for him. Who thought of that?

It's the name he came with, Oren said quietly. From a shelter in Boston.

Boomerang would have been a better name, I whispered.

The vet smiled and touched my arm. So he'd come back?

I stared at the vet. She thought I was a good person.

Oren had planned on going in to work later that afternoon, but in retrospect, this was unrealistic. Instead we drove to City Beach and walked along the cement path near the fish restaurant. It was blustery, and we crossed our arms over our chests. One of us would attempt to make conversation about salad or Thailand, but this was also unrealistic, since the only thing we could think about was the cat. At one point I told Oren that Fiona hated me, but he disagreed. She hardly knows you, Edie. You're just feeling sad.

That night I talked in my sleep. Oren said I sat straight up in bed and said very clearly, Practice dying to fall asleep.

33

He was standing in line at the bakery, across the street from the advertising agency. I had paused in the shade to yank the back of my sock out of my shoe. I was on the way home from buying local honey and nutritional yeast at the health food store. The sound of men loudly greeting each other caused me to glance over.

Vincent Guerra, #1 in Real Estate, looked different from his posters, in that his shirt was not ripped open to expose the torso of a muscular green superhero, his legs were not chess pieces, and his hands were not made of sharp metal. He was wearing a bright blue suit and brown shoes, like he was dressed for a summer wedding. His face, however, was unmistakable. From across the street, I could see the whiteness of his teeth and the sun reflecting off his tan skin. His hair was black and in stiff waves, like a piece of new car tire. He shook hands with a man whose loud show-offy voice suggested they barely knew each other. The two spoke until the line moved forward and the loud man said goodbye and Vincent disappeared inside.

I felt dizzy. I sat on a nearby bench and kept my eyes on the bakery. Seeing Vincent lit something inside me. Every one of this greedy slimeball's ads flashed across my brain like neon lights. My knees began to tremble and I dropped my bag. My eyes burned. All I could think about were all the bullshit stories and pictures and taglines. The ways we deceive each other with phony fucking phrases that grow in our brains like tumors. The stupid ways we dress ourselves and feed ourselves and pretend we are more than animals. He was in there right now, chatting with the women behind the counter, asking them what's fresh or whether he should splurge on a vanilla slice. I thought about the glass bottle of honey in my grocery bag and how far I could throw it.

I sat motionless until he walked out of the bakery, squinting at the sunlight, holding something wrapped in white paper. He pulled out a pair of dark glasses from his jacket pocket and put them on as he walked briskly up the street, past round tables of coffee drinkers and past the shop that sold expensive bath soap and welcome mats. I began walking in the same direction, away from home. He held his package like a clutch purse and took wide steps as if he were avoiding cracks, nodding at passersby. At the intersection he turned left, so I crossed the street and soon was following him down the tree-lined residential block. He stopped next to a red sports car and reached his hand in his pocket.

He was going to drive away.

I sprinted, leaping the last few steps and landing directly in front of him as he reached for the handle of his car. He let out a yelp. I had surprised him.

May I help you? he asked. His voice was higher than I expected. I stared at him. Are you ok? he said.

I took a deep breath, swung my tote bag over my shoulder, shoved my hands in my fleece vest pockets, and said, Why do you have those ads plastered all over the city?

His white teeth shone. Ah, you recognize me, he said. Sorry about that. It's a bit obnoxious I reckon, but it's good for business. He laughed.

Doesn't it drive you crazy? Seeing yourself on huge billboards? You're everywhere, I said, yanking a stray hair out of my mouth.

Six, he said.

What?

There are six billboards. Are you Canadian?

It seems like more, I said.

He paused and glanced at his white paper package from the bakery. Is there something I can help you with? I have a sandwich here. I'm on my way to a meeting.

I just don't know why you'd go to all that trouble to make ads that are so awful. Don't you want to connect with people more? Like, show them you're an actual human being? My voice had become shrill and unstable. I mean, a chess piece? The Incredible Hulk?

He raised his hand defensively. Hey, hold on. No need to get so angry. To be honest, those are the ads that bring in customers. I know they're tacky, but I reckon they work.

He wasn't angry. Why wasn't he angry?

I suddenly felt an enormous swelling in my chest, as if someone had ripped out my anger, reshaped it into another emotion entirely, and stuffed it back in my body. My eyes filled with tears.

He put his keys back in his pocket and touched my shoulder. Are you ok? he said. He wore cologne from the 1990s, the sort that would come in a blue bottle to convey a sense of seamanship.

No, I said quietly, looking at the ground. I am not ok.

Several large anthills made the sidewalk look like the surface of the moon.

Would you like to sit down? He gestured to the front steps of a small brick house with a tiny green lawn and two small metal rabbits. A fairy-tale house. Let's sit down, he said.

Can I call anyone for you? he asked, now sitting next to me on the stair, putting his sandwich beside him. The sun was bright and I could see two of me in his glasses. I shook my head.

No thank you, I said quietly. I didn't know why I was crying, nor why I had followed him. This was all bad.

I took a deep breath and said slowly, I killed my father.

Pardon? His voice got quiet.

I rested my elbows on my knees, clasped my hands, and turned to him. My father, I said. I killed my father. I held my breath as my eyes burned from melting-hot sunscreen.

Suddenly there were three of us. I felt like I could see the thing I had just released, standing on the sidewalk, shaking its head, mouth agape, waiting. The thing and Vincent stayed silent while I cried.

I cried for a long time. Across the street, two teenagers stopped and stared at me before Vincent waved them on.

Finally, Vincent removed his sunglasses, folded them carefully, and placed them between us on the stair. He sat frozen. With his mouth closed and teeth hidden, his face looked softer.

We sat together not speaking for a few minutes while I took short breaths, as if collecting small pieces of air. I had never cried like this before. My lungs had to reconstruct themselves.

People don't just go around killing each other, Vincent finally said confidently. After a brief pause he added quietly, Are you sure you don't want me to call someone? I'm not really sure what to do here. It seems like we should call someone.

I shook my head and wiped my nose with the back of my hand. My eyes burned and my throat was dry. He had Alzheimer's, I said.

Vincent sighed and said, I'm sorry. I'm familiar with that. Mum had something like that. We lost her a few years back.

He unwrapped his sandwich and pulled out a white paper napkin that he handed to me.

Thank you, I mumbled.

He looked at the sky and continued to speak. It's the kind of thing you don't get over, do you? Watching someone you love fall apart. I can be having a normal day, everything's good, and then bam—he smashed his fist into his palm—you remember something like Mum crying out or asking who you are. Mum was screaming at everyone for a while. That might have been the hardest.

He shook his head, remembering.

She was a terrific person, really strong. Did everything for us kids, you know. It's not natural, the mind diseases. Physical ones you expect, you can plan for. You can't exactly get a wheelchair ramp for the brain, I reckon. You know what I mean? And the way it changes all the time. One minute she's cooking your favorite dish, then all of a sudden she's pulling the hairs out of her arms.

I burst out crying and said, I put a t-shirt over his mouth and suffocated him.

I blurted this out like a poison arrow. I couldn't take it back.

Oh god, he said, pressing his thumb and index finger into the inside corners of his eye sockets. A dog barked as a gray car drove by. His fingers stayed pushing on his eyes for a while as I continued to cry. The sun beat down. A woman walked by glancing sideways at us. I stared at the sidewalk, wishing it would suck me in.

He held the side of his finger to his nose as if trying to stop a sneeze and shook his head back and forth. I don't know what to say, he said finally, sitting up straight. Why are you telling me this?

I don't know, I said quietly, wiping the corners of my mouth where my lip gloss had accumulated. I didn't mean to. I just saw you and then followed you, and then it came out.

He asked me when it had happened, and I said over a year ago and added that I had moved to Perth with my husband soon after.

So your husband knows, he said.

I shook my head.

He sighed and scraped something off the side of his shoe with his fingernail. He wore a gold wedding band. He stuck his foot out in front of him, looked at it, sighed again, and said, It's not something I really want to be a part of.

He looked at me and said, I don't mean to be cruel. I just don't know you. And this doesn't seem like something I should get involved with. You know what I'm saying?

I nodded and said, You don't need to do anything. I'm sorry. I don't know why I told you.

A magpie landed on the small lawn between the two metal rabbits. It looked at one rabbit and then hopped over to the other and found a crumb on the grass.

He said, I reckon you told me because you needed to tell someone. If what you're saying is true, then it is certainly too big to be contained within one person.

He looked at the magpie and continued. I am not a religious person in any sense of the word, but this is why Catholics have confession. You can't possibly be expected to hold that kind of thing inside forever. If you ask me, this is one of the major benefits of having a partner. We're not meant to be alone. Life throws us all sorts of shit. It's a lot to handle. If I couldn't talk to my partner, I'd fucking explode. Sorry, but it's true.

The magpie looked at me and flew to the top of a parking sign. Vincent said, I'm sure you had your reasons. You must have had a reason. He paused, rubbed his temple, and looked at me. You had a reason, right?

I didn't know anymore. The thing had been released, and everything was different now. It's like I had been split in half and could not be put back together the way I was.

I don't know about a reason, I said. I don't know.

He asked if my husband was at home and I said he would be home later that night. He offered to stay with me until he got back but I said no thanks.

Don't you have a meeting? I said.

He shrugged his shoulders. I lied, he said. I was hungry. He looked down at his sandwich. Sorry about that.

Vincent drove me home in his red sports car. As I was getting out, he said, Hey, I'm sorry about all those ads. He looked down at the steering wheel and said quietly, At least you know where to find me.

34

I ate beef jerky and a bowl of cereal for dinner and fell asleep before Oren got home.

The next morning, as Oren stood in front of the bedroom mirror running his fingers through his hair repeatedly and aggressively like a cat covering up pee, he asked me if anything was wrong.

I was in bed, with a book of poetry by Edna St. Vincent Millay. Oren had suggested I read a poem every morning. It might help you calibrate, he had said. I hadn't heard Oren use the word *calibrate* before. He must have read an article.

This morning's poem was "Dirge without Music," which began, *I am not resigned to the shutting away of loving hearts in the hard ground.*

I told him poems about death first thing in the morning didn't seem like the best way to calibrate. I tossed the book next to me on the bed, rubbed my eyes, and said softly, No one loves me in the way I want to be loved.

He pulled a belt through his pant loops and asked me how exactly did I want to be loved then. For the love of god, he said, how should I love you?

I don't know, I said.

Without saying anything, he slowly rolled his cuffs up to his elbows. Finally he looked at me and asked, Do you even want to be loved?

I don't know.

Well, lucky for you, he said, standing over me sternly, you don't get to choose that. You don't get to decide who loves you.

His face was turning red.

He said, People are going to come into your life and they are going to love you. Tough shit. You don't have to listen to them. You don't have to keep them around. You might not even meet them in the first place. But they will love you. Like I love you.

He paced back and forth at the foot of the bed.

You are terrible sometimes, you know that? Callous, self-centered, terrible. A classic case of emotional immaturity.

Where had he gotten that expression?

But I love you and I'm sorry it's not in the special way you think you need, but let me tell you something. You married me and I love you in the way that I love my wife. If you don't want to be here anymore, leave. Whatever.

I watched him walk back and forth. I had never seen Oren like this.

He pointed at me. Stop moping around saying no one loves you in the perfect way you need to be loved. You don't get to make that call. I decide how I love you, he said, smacking his chest. I decide. And right now, to be honest with you, I feel like I'm running out of love. I've been tiptoeing around you for months now, and I'm sick of it.

He waited for me to respond, but I had nothing to say.

I'm scared of you, Edie. That's the truth. I try so hard to not upset you, to let you do your own thing, but I can't take it anymore. There's obviously something going on with you. There has been for a while now. At first I thought it was the move. Or your dad. But lately I have no idea what's going on. You're closed off, and testy, and eating weird shit, and just, I don't know, cruel.

He looked at me and said, You're cruel, Edie.

I blinked.

He pulled his brown leather dress shoes out of the closet and sat down on the bed, shaking his head. He tied his shoes violently and stood up, yanking down his pant legs.

I'm cruel, I said quietly.

Oren ignored me. I'm going to work, he said. I'm going to work so I can make money for the woman I love in a way that makes her miserable, and then I'm going to come home and you're going to tell me what the fuck your actual problem is. No more of this I-don't-love-you-right crap. Tell me what's wrong.

I sat up on my elbows. I smelled like old salad.

He glared at me. You're going to tell me what the hell is wrong with you, he said. And I don't mean in general, I mean very specifically, Edie.

He looked at his phone and said, I gotta go. The bus is coming. He ran down the hall and slammed the door.

I rolled over and buried my head in Oren's pillow, smelling him, glad he was gone but wishing he hadn't left me alone. I lay back down and closed my eyes. I thought of Abby and then of Vincent. I heard a repetitive banging and opened my eyes. A magpie was throwing itself against the bedroom window over and over again. Banging itself against the glass.

I squeezed my eyes shut. The banging continued. I imagined the magpie growing larger and larger, crashing through the window and landing on my bed in a pile of shattered glass. It would use its monstrous claws to pick me up by the ankles and then it would shout, Look at you. Look at how little you are doing and how much it feels like everything and nothing. I would scream and try to kick my legs free. Its claws would tighten around my ankles and it would fly me from room to room, banging my body into walls, smashing me against closet doors, using my head to sweep wineglasses and picture frames off shelves. Twisting me from side to side, forcing me to face the wreckage.

With my eyes closed, I could see the bird's enormous black holes for eyes. I began to cry.

My thoughts swirled. *What am I supposed to do now? I can't do anything about it. Is that what you wanted? Is that it? To show me what I've done? To prove that I ruined something? What did I ruin? How could I have possibly ruined anything? It was gone already. He was gone already. What was I supposed to do? Wait for him to die alone? That would have been cruel.*

My body tightened and then rocked from side to side, finally falling off the bed. I opened my eyes. Crumpled on the bedroom floor sobbing, I searched for broken glass but only saw my hands spread wide on the rug. I closed my eyes and saw the magpie. I opened them and saw my hands, displayed like evidence. My thumbs wiggled and felt the roughness of the rug, the opposite of skin and of soft, slow, dying breath. Sitting back on my heels, I traced my thumbs along the tips of my fingers. One, two, three, four. And back. Four, three, two, one.

I found a blue pen on the floor, under the bed. I flicked it open, then closed, the tiny head of the pen appearing and disappearing. I tried to focus on the up and down, the predictability of something.

Dad.

I felt a sharp pain in my stomach and doubled over, head to my knees. Breathing made the pain swell up and over my back. I clutched the pen in one hand and the backs of my thighs with the other. I tried to think about the lake and the birds, but then I smelled sausage and eucalyptus and soon felt dizzy.

I crawled to the bathroom and opened the bottom drawer where Oren kept a bottle of muscle relaxants from an old car accident. I swallowed as many as I could without water. Three. Four.

*

I woke up on the floor with rug burn on my cheek. It was getting dark outside. I had slept all day. Oren might be home soon. I walked carefully to the kitchen for a glass of water and saw the time glowing above the oven.

Where is he?

I ran outside. There at the foot of a thorny bush was the possum.

Epilogue

The fresh corpse is swinging from your hand as you run next door and up the seven cement steps of Fiona's house.

Breathing heavily, you stand in front of her front door, clenching the corpse. Through the panel of rose-red stained glass, you spot a silhouette pass from one room to another. Fiona, or her husband, or maybe the girl. You inhale sharply, turn to look at the animal hanging from your hand, change your mind, and run down the seven steps to turn the corner to the large side window that overlooks your house.

With all of your strength, you hurl the corpse of the dead possum toward Fiona's house. It thumps against the window and slides down, leaving a dark brown bloody smear before dropping in the dirt. A man's voice coming from inside yells, What the hell? and you reach over the bush to find the animal, this time grabbing the torso because there isn't time to find the tail. Your fingers sink into the hair and grab on to the body with desperation, like you are hanging off a cliff. You pull it back, over your right shoulder, and heave it harder this time.

The corpse shatters the window. The sound of glass exploding is exhilarating. Fireworks. For a brief moment, something in you is illuminated and healed. This is temporary of course. You have done something barbaric.

A girl screams. A mother screams, What is that? A baby cries. A father screams, What the hell? and now *what the hell* is louder as he flings open the front door and runs down the seven steps and around the corner, where in front of him he sees his American neighbor in a black dress, with dirt on her face and arms, kneeling on the ground. What the hell? he screams again.

He uses your name this time. Edie? He rests his hand on your shoulder for a moment, because he doesn't yet know all the facts and is concerned you are hurt. He is gathering information and is not someone who is quick to blame. It is dark outside, which makes it more difficult to understand what has happened. The father looks at the detonated window, the gaping hole in his house, the very house he himself was raised in, and looks back down at you. Still he does not understand. You are seemingly frozen, kneeling in the dirt, looking at your hands resting on your thighs.

Like an ambulance, a girl's piercing shriek enters the scene. He's dead, the girl inside cries. The father whips around and runs, tackling the stairs in two giant leaps. She screams again, He's dead, Daddy, he's on the floor. You hear the mother and father exchange words. They are talking about the dead possum that has crashed through their window.

Fiona runs toward you. She is in gray leggings and an off-shoulder pastel blue t-shirt, and her blond hair is tangled and wild. With both of her hands, she pushes you to the ground. What the bloody fuck, Edie? What the fuck is your problem? You could have killed someone, you fucking psycho. She kneels over you, grabs your wrists and tries to pull them away from your face. Her hair is brushing against your head. You cover your eyes and draw your knees up to your chest. You can feel scraping on your lower back because your dress is above your waist, twisted around your body like shedding skin. She screams in your face that you are a fucking psychopath. That you could have killed someone with whatever the fuck that thing is, oh my god, was that a dead animal, you bitch? And broken glass, Edie, do you have any idea what you did? Glass is everywhere. We have a baby, Edie. What the hell is wrong with you?

You hear the girl crying inside the house. Daddy, what is it? Daddy! Is it a possum?

Fiona shakes you by the shoulders. Edie?

You shriek, Get away from me. Leave me alone. You kick your legs and twist from side to side.

Fiona is a mother, indifferent to a tantrum, and slaps you across the face. Leave you alone? You threw an animal through my kitchen window. You broke the window and now there's a dead fucking animal in our house.

You don't get it, you scream. You don't get *this*!

Her blue eyes get big. She is furious. You could have killed someone, Edie!

You shove your knee into Fiona's chin, not to hurt her, but to get her out of your face. She howls and falls back. You roll to one side and pull up your knees as tightly as you can. The sound that comes out of your mouth begins like a distant foghorn and becomes the howl of a wounded animal.

An ibis lands on the ground nearby.

Edie?

Oren is here now.

Edie, Oren says gravely. What have you done?

His voice pulls you back to this moment. He has come home to an appalling sight, to find his wife next door in the dirt, with a broken window nearby and a family in chaos. By now, neighbors have congregated on the dark suburban street. Fiona yells at Oren that his wife did something psychotic, and he yells back at her to shut up, to shut the fuck up already. He wants to talk to Edie. He is sorry.

You're late, you say, your red face buried in your arms.

Edie, he says, rolling you over to face him. What happened? What did you do?

Your swollen eyes fill with tears and you take a deep breath. The night air comes up through your lungs and out your mouth like invisible lava. Your face and the face of your husband are almost touching.

The sun has set, the mosquitos are out, and you are collapsed in the grass, crying, your sundress twisted and stained with mud. Fiona is crying. Her window has been smashed, putting her family in danger. A dead possum is sprawled on the floor of her house.

Your husband holds your head in his hands and traces his thumbs over your eyebrows. He stares at you. Edie, everyone's freaking out. Tell me what happened.

You feel a bug crawl across your hairline, and you shake your head back and forth. You remember a movie you once watched with your family. Filmmakers had strapped tiny cameras to the backs of insects. Your father said there are things that humans will never understand but they will never stop trying. His brown eyes sparkled when he said that, and this memory now makes your chest hurt.

Above Oren's head, the clouds are moving fast across the sky. Green leaves sway gently. Inside each leaf are small breathing tubes. *Stomata*, you think you remember from high school science. Greek for "mouth." Hundreds of thousands of tiny breathing systems all around you.

You think about everything that breathes, and how we are all floating through space like cosmic dandruff. Your heart is racing.

You killed your father because you wanted to.

Every day you imagine a life without Oren. Every single day.

He is crouched next to you now.

Your crying becomes a monsoon because it cannot be any other way. This is the cry of someone in a story who is changing. This messy, loud, torrential rupture is the declaration of a shift. Your husband is startled. He has never seen you like this. He knows he has never known all of you but decided years ago that this was enough. He has loved you from the beginning. You try to sit up, but your body is stiff and heavy and falls back to the ground. You can no longer see Oren clearly through your tears, so you throw your head back and reach your arm straight up as if stuck in an icy pond. Pull me out of this, you want to say, but you can't form any words. He takes your arm and holds on tight.

Two hundred and six bones in the human body.

I got you, he says, and kisses the crease of your elbow.

You try to inhale and it feels like staccato notes piercing you in the chest. It is like you are breathing in sharp needles, like your breathing is climbing over barbed wire. Finally, you manage to release the words: I killed him.

A crow howls. I killed him, you repeat, louder this time. And then you can't stop saying it. I killed him. Louder and louder.

Fiona yells, And now it's in our fucking house!

Everyone thinks you mean the possum.

Your husband pulls you to a sitting position and leans you against him. Edie. Look at me.

You raise your head. Your face is soaking wet, snot is pouring from your nostrils. I killed him, you say.

I'm here, Edie, he says quietly. Do you see me?

You nod. He places his hand on your knee and squeezes it. It is the most perfect touch that has ever occurred in the history of human-kind. You feel cradled and pushed up and over something. You have never been completely alone.

You glance at a cockroach in the grass. You open your mouth and, trembling, say, I'm sorry I haven't been the easiest person.

Your husband nods. He needed to hear this. He bumps into your side and says, I wasn't looking for the easiest.

Come on, Edie, he says. Let's get you inside. He smacks his ankle.

He pulls you to a standing position. Fiona runs over and grabs Oren's arm. What are we supposed to do now? She nearly killed us!

Oren whips around and in a voice both firm and kind says, Fiona, we are very sorry. We will pay for all damages and help with the clean-up. But right now, I need to take her inside. He gestures toward you. Fiona looks at you and then back at Oren. She shakes her head and storms back to her house.

You know that after you walk through the door, Oren will lead you to the bedroom, blast the air-conditioning, and suggest you change your clothes. He will also change. Then he will get two glasses of water and come back to the bedroom. By this time, you will have managed to get yourself out of the sundress and under the covers. He will sit next to you and make attempts to calm you with stories about his Japanese coworker with the pink elephant backpack and the ergonomics workshop he was forced to attend. Then, cautiously, he will ask you again what happened tonight, and you will take a deep breath and say that actually you want to talk about something else.

Acknowledgments

I completed the first draft of *Edie Richter is Not Alone* at the Nedlands Library in Perth and made the final edits at my home in San Francisco during a global pandemic.

I am immensely grateful to the following people:

Susan Midalia, for believing in Edie and for the first line of chapter five, borrowed with permission from her short story "Oranges"

Daniel Handler, Sandra Handler, and the late Louis Handler

Lisa Brown and Otto Handler

The Andrades and the Outlaws

Alex Elite, Sarah Kennedy, Aaron Sheddrick, and Harlan Kennedy

Druimé Nolan and Ben Carlish

Christina Liew, Christina McLeish, Racquel Sanderson, and the Wilkes family

The late Beate Mohr

Andrew Sean Greer, Caroline Paul, and Dana Reinhardt

Rita Bullwinkel, Lauren Cerand, and Katherine Firth

Readers of onewomanparty.com

Hospice workers everywhere

Steven Salpeter at Curtis Brown

Chris Heiser, Olivia Taylor Smith, Jaya Nicely, and everyone at Unnamed Press

Willa and Simone, I love being your mom.

David Andrade, thank you for being my brilliant first reader and editor. You belong to everyone, but I'm so happy you're mine.